SIST

The Garden of Eden—that's Sister Eve
Carrol's first impression of the plantation
hospital in Malaysia. But she soon un-
covers problems in paradise when she
incurs the displeasure of her handsome
boss, Dr Andrew Craig . . .

SISTER IN A SARONG

BY

JENNY ASHE

MILLS & BOON LIMITED
15–16 BROOK'S MEWS
LONDON W1A 1DR

First published in Great Britain 1984
by Mills & Boon Limited

© Jenny Ashe 1984

Australian copyright 1984
Philippine copyright 1984

ISBN 0 263 74963 0

Set in 10 on 11½ pt Linotron Times
03–0285–55,500

Photoset by Rowland Phototypesetting Ltd
Bury St Edmunds, Suffolk
Made and printed in Great Britain by
Richard Clay (The Chaucer Press) Ltd
Bungay, Suffolk

CHAPTER ONE

EVE CARROL crashed the gears wearily as her elderly van protested at yet another rise in the muddy jungle road. It was getting dark and the high trees were closing in over her head, the creature noises in the thickets becoming menacing and strange. It could not be far now to the village of Dantang, and Eve would prefer not to get lost at this stage of her journey.

She narrowed her eyes, trying to see some hint of light in the distance. But the road wound through the trees, and it was all she could do to see in the light of her headlights where it twisted through the tall palms at the edge of the jungle. Why did night always fall so fast in Malaysia? The van squelched through a large wet hole, and mud splodged up over the windscreen. She dare not stop to clean it off. She was low on gas and she must try to keep up a steady pace, to economise, until she could fill up the tank at Dantang village kampong.

Eve brushed her eyes with the back of her hand. Her hair was damp with sweat over her forehead, and the thought of a cool shower was sweet in her mind. She hoped the facilities at the Plantation Hospital were not too primitive. Eve was no stranger to roughing it, but she had been living easy in Kuala Lumpur. The nurses' home there had been like a five-star hotel. She would prefer not to have to sample the opposite.

Just then the road ahead brightened a little. For a second, she thought she had arrived. Then she realised the light was from the headlights of some vehicle behind her. Her heart missed a beat. It was a lonely road. And her friends in KL had teased her about stories of bandits who lived in the jungle, bands of outlaws, left over from the days of the Communist terrorists.

Eve gritted her teeth and kept her foot on the accelerator. The lights were closing. Suddenly there was an insolent beep on a rather expensive horn, and she found herself overtaken and splashed by a long sleek limousine. In her own headlights she saw the dark outline of the driver, a tall man with his head thrown back at an arrogant angle, as his car purred on round a bend and out of sight in a moment.

There was a sharp jerk, and Eve's angry comments were forgotten as one wheel lodged firmly in a pot-hole. It was night now, and the forest around her seemed impenetrable. Yet the sky above, where she could see it between fronded palms and gnarled black branches, was a tender soft blue, with a luminous sheen from the rays of a fast-setting sun at some invisible horizon. A single star flickered briefly as Eve turned her attention to roaring the van backwards to bounce the wheel from the hole. At first it stayed fixed stubbornly, the wheel spinning messily in the mud as she pressed the accelerator. She set her lips firmly together. Eve was not a girl to let things beat her. She switched off the engine and paused to think.

If only that road-hog had come along now. She had a torch, and she groped for it in the back of the van. But was there any point getting out in all that mud, just to look at a pot-hole? In the sudden quiet, without the drone of the engine, the noises of the jungle closed in. And the squeaks, whistles and chatterings were enough to discourage any evening strolls. The night crickets whirred their strident chorus all around her. Eve shivered in spite of the clammy heat and shrugged her shoulders as she turned the key again. As though it had been teasing her, the engine started, and as she pushed the gear into first, the old van eased itself with a bounce out of the hole and began to jolt and wobble along the road to Dantang.

Then she saw light ahead. Eve could hardly restrain herself from giving a whoop of joy, almost as loud as the coppersmith birds she heard in the trees. A great owl swooped for its prey just in front of her, like a mop-head dropped from a skyscraper. 'Dantang, here I come.' She speeded up, towards the welcoming glow in the distance.

As she neared the lights, she saw not a village, but a battered gas station among the trees. It looked like fairyland, with naked coloured bulbs strung up around the shabby little cabin, as though on a Christmas tree, lighting up three ancient petrol pumps. The van coughed, jerked, and lurched like a drunken man into the muddy forecourt.

A plump Malay was reading a comic in the kiosk. He looked up at the sound of a customer, and his narrow slit eyes opened slightly wider in astonishment. Eve smiled to herself. She must look like some scruffy schoolgirl, rather than the cool, qualified Sister that she was, in her muddy shorts, striped tee-shirt and sandals hidden by the grime and dirt of a far from comfortable journey. Her fair curls clung to her head with sweat, and her face must be streaked with mud, where she had wiped the perspiration from running into her eyes.

In her best Malay, Eve said, '*Salaam*. This is Dantang? I am the new Sister for the hospital. Please fill up my van with gasolene.' She knew her accent was poor, but she must practise as much as possible. Many of her patients would speak only Malay.

'You English?' He was not unwelcoming. He put his comic down and Eve saw with a shock that it was pornographic, with drawings of unclad females, done by someone with a poor knowledge of anatomy. She averted her eyes, and indicated the petrol pumps. The Malay shook his head. 'Very sorry, no gas. Delivery truck not get through today. Come tomorrow.'

'Oh, no.' Eve hesitated. She looked at the van, pathetic in its mud. 'Is it far to the hospital?'

'Not far.' He heaved himself down from his wooden cabin. He wore a vest with a hole in it, and a greasy sarong slung round his ample middle. His feet were bare. But his manner was helpful, and he spoke English. 'You want push van round back? I help. Come, *lah*.'

'Okay. Thanks, I mean *terimasakih*. I can walk the rest of the way and come back for my things in the morning.' But Eve looked around rather apprehensively. She could see no more lights among the trees. It looked as though there was only this tiny bright place in the whole black jungle. But then she heard a welcome sound—the yapping of domestic dogs. The village could not be far, after all. Then she heard a child's cry and, through the night, the gentle clucking of scavenging chickens. She had reached Dantang. She nodded at the Malay. 'I'll come back tomorrow.'

He grinned, and his eyes almost disappeared in the two round globes of his cheeks. He was looking distinctly pleased, and Eve realised with a jolt that he was staring at her bare legs. She remembered the pictures in his comic and hastily turned to get her shoulder-bag from the van and lock the doors. The Malay said, 'My name is Abbas. I keep this place, and my wife, she keep bazaar. You come tomorrow, buy many things you need, *lah*? Anything you want, we help. No trouble, okay?'

She nodded, more than ready to go. 'You've been very kind. Which way is the hospital?'

He stepped closer, putting an oily hand on her

shoulder while he pointed the way with the other. Eve tried not to squirm. Hie breath smelt of garlic, and his fingers of engine oil.

There was a roar in the jungle, and Eve thought at first that it was yet another strange animal noise. But it became louder, and Abbas let go of her and turned towards the road. It was a car, an automatic changing gear to make it up the last steep stretch of road. 'Tuan Doctor. It is Dr Craig. He is going to hospital, *lah*.' The grin was back. 'No need to walk, Sister.' His bland face took on an obsequious expression, his head tilted to one side, his hands rubbing together. A sleek green Rover emerged into the circle of light cast by the string of electric bulbs between the mud-spattered palms.

The Rover crawled elegantly into the gas station and drew up by the pumps. 'Evening, Abbas. Fill her up, please. How's the baby?' A dark brown, cultured voice. And the man who opened the car door to hand Abbas the key, fitted the voice. He was tall, with broad shoulders and narrow hips. He was expensively dressed in tailored shirt and slacks, the creases immaculate.

Eve found herself staring. So this was Andrew Craig, the man she had come to work for. And it was the car, she was sure, that had overtaken her near that pot-hole. So why was he here after she was? She had not passed him. She looked at the tall figure with curiosity, and a little annoyance at his rudeness in overtaking her so fast. She would enjoy seeing this rather arrogant man taken down a peg when he was told there was no petrol.

But the Malay was hurrying to the pump. He took the key from the doctor and opened the cap. Then he proceeded to insert the pump and re-fuel the Rover. Eve felt the fury rise within her. The man from the Rover stood erect, not noticing her. She noticed his mass of dark wavy hair, tendrils curling over the crisp collar of his shirt. She said in a low voice to Abbas, 'I thought you had no petrol. What kind of low-down trick is that? You only sell to rich men, is that it?'

She had spoken quietly, though angrily. The doctor turned round. She saw fierce black eyes under heavy brows, an aristocratic nose, a square angular jaw, set in a way that brooked no opposition. A man used to being obeyed. A hard man. A man Eve did not care for. His gaze was rather too long, thorough. She saw his glance shift to the girlie magazine Abbas had put down. Then the dark eyes raked her scanty shorts, her dishevelled appearance, and made her feel like something unclean, something one notices in the gutter and does not look at again. Sweat began to run down her face into her eyes, and she felt her breathing become faster in her anger and frustration.

The Malay introduced them quickly, hoping to divert Eve's wrath from his own mean trick with the petrol. 'This is new Sister for hospital, Tuan Doctor.' Andrew Craig looked again in Eve's direction, and when their eyes met it was like the clash of steel on steel. Her blue eyes could be as hard as his, and her nature was not to give in to rudeness. Abbas had hoped to start a friendship. But here was no hint of fellowship, of welcome, no comradeship of two Britons in a foreign country, two medical people here to dedicate themselves to people who needed them. Firm, unyielding coolness on both sides was all the little garage man saw. Dr Craig bent his head a millimetre. 'Sister Carrol.'

She said as little as possible. 'How do you do, Dr Craig.'

'You have some trouble?' He didn't sound as though he cared a scrap.

'Only a tiring journey from KL. And the miracle of the petrol pump that was empty until you came along.'

Now her irritation involved both men, and Abbas took a couple of steps backwards. Eve shook her head wearily.

The doctor looked casually at the van. 'You didn't have to travel alone. We usually lay on transport for our staff.' He was implying it was all her own fault. Abbas hastily screwed the cap back on the Rover and locked it. Craig towered over the Malay and Eve, not only in size, but in physical personality and professional superiority. 'However, I can take you along. I am going to the hospital.'

Eve looked at Abbas, still furious. 'You daren't tell me you still have no gas?'

The Malay shrugged. 'Tuan Doctor had the last.'

Eve turned back to Dr Craig. The disdainful face might have been handsome, she thought, if it had shown one spark of humanity. 'I seem to have no choice. I do apologise for troubling you.' Her voice was cold.

The noises of the jungle had become less savage than the conversation in the gas station. Abbas merged hastily into the background, hoping to escape further involvement. At that moment there was a sharp crackling noise out among the trees, and the two protagonists turned quickly in that direction. A clatter of birds' wings followed the sound, and an acceleration of the jungle screams and whistles. Then there was another whistle, long and drawn out.

Dr Craig drew in his breath and suddenly strode away from them, into the blackness of the jungle. She heard his footsteps, treading on small twigs in the undergrowth. Then there was nothing—no human sound at all. He had been absorbed into the mystery of the jungle. Eve waited, holding her breath, in the unearthly circle of anonymous sounds. Surely she was wrong? It could not have been gunfire, could it? Yet she had seen too many war films not to recognise the sound.

Abbas too was staring into the blackness. Eve said, 'Do you often hear that?'

Abbas shrugged plump shoulders. 'Sometimes. Better take no notice.'

'But what is it? Who is it?' He did not answer. 'And where has your precious Tuan Doctor gone now?'

He smiled at her, a mysterious smile that meant he was saying no more. Eve felt afraid. 'Are there still bandits here?' Her friends had not been joking, then. It must be true. Abbas returned to his kiosk and pretended to be reading his comic. Eve looked around again. She had come here to work at a village hospital, to look after the rubber plantation workers. She expected to look after child welfare, cuts and bruises, infections and stings, malnutrition due to ignorance. She had not come here to treat bullet wounds.

'Come along, Sister Carrol. Hurry up. You do want to get to the hospital before midnight, I suppose?' Dr Craig was back, and his long legs took him swiftly to the Rover, where he waited for Eve to catch up. She was annoyed with herself for being relieved to see him. He did not offer to help with her luggage, so she took only her shoulder-bag and one case. She could collect the other tomorrow, when she came for her van. Dr Craig glanced with a thinly veiled disapproval at her smeared tee-shirt and muddy feet as she sat in the passenger seat, and then looked away without speaking.

Eve said, 'That was gunfire.'

She waited. Dr Craig started the car. Then he said calmly, 'Only to be expected. Nothing to worry about. The army has a range near here. A practice range.'

Eve was only half satisfied. Abbas had not told her that. And this was a funny time to be practising. She sat back as the Rover purred its way out of the circle of light, into the mass of trees ahead, lit now by headlights on full beam. The strange shapes of the fronded jungle leaves, the great floppy banana leaves, spiked plants, seemed to part and separate, as the limousine moved unerringly through them.

Eve smelt the sweet fragrance of woodsmoke and heard again the yapping of the dogs. They saw a dimly lit group of wooden houses. 'Is that Dantang?'

'Part of it. It's a sprawling little place.' Dr Craig pointed to the other side of the path. 'That is the rubber plantation. Most of our patients work there. They are quite prosperous by peasant standards.' Eve looked, and saw shadowy trunks, straight and regimented, like soldiers in lines. Along the edge of the road were tall grasses and more shrubs with pointing leaves, like bunches of upright swords.

'You live at the hospital, do you, Dr Craig?' Eve found that some of her animosity had faded, in the interest in her surroundings, at the thought of working here for two years.

'Only occasionally. I have three other hospitals to supervise in the area. I stay when necessary.' And from his voice Eve read that it would be beneath his dignity to stay in the same place as the disreputable waif at his side.

She said no more. She was here to do a job that she had wanted to do for years. She intended to enjoy it, in spite of Andrew Craig. Suddenly the car began to slow down and they swayed as he braked. 'Here we are.'

In front of them was an oasis of light. There was a wooden veranda, covered in creepers and climbing orchids. A metal bridge led from the parking space across a deep monsoon drain to the steps up to the veranda and an open front door, covered with a thin muslin mosquito curtain. She saw a table spread with a white cloth. A fan revolved gently in the ceiling, and a slim figure in a dark blue sarong was placing plates and cups on the table. Craig hooted the horn. This time it did not sound insolent.

For a moment nothing happened, and Eve had the strange feeling that this lovely, comfortable scene was only a mirage, suspended in time and space, and that as soon as she got out of the car it would disappear into the jungle. She collected her bags and climbed out into a clearing of springy, sweet-smelling grass.

Dantang Plantation Hospital did not disappear. Instead, the neat figure in the sarong, with shining black hair piled up in an elaborate chignon, came smiling to the door. She looked stunning, like some high society hostess.

'Sister Carrol, how nice to meet you at last.' Her English was almost perfect. 'I was getting a little worried.' Her voice was like tinkling Chinese music. She held out her hand, and the two women smiled at each other as they shook hands.

'I'm rather muddy, I'm afraid. Had a bit of bother with a pot-hole on the way. Then I ran out of gas, and Abbas wouldn't let me have any.' Eve tried not to sound cross. 'You must be Lisa Kai. I've been looking forward to working here.'

The Malay girl smiled. 'Abbas is a law unto himself. I'll tell you about all our eccentrics when you have made yourself comfortable and had a good meal.' She insisted on taking Eve's suitcase, and led the way into the comfortable room up the three wooden steps to the veranda. Eve sensed that the welcome was genuine, and warmed towards the gentle girl with the trim figure and pretty voice.

'Is there a cup of tea, Lisa?' Dr Craig's hard voice had mellowed, as though even he could not speak to this hospitable soul without equal courtesy. Eve watched him. Once he showed a spark of humanity, his face was attractive and handsome, not the previous sardonic mask she had noticed when they first met. So he can be human after all, she thought wryly, when the woman is pretty enough.

'Of course.' Lisa laughed as she crossed the room to where a kettle hissed on a small spirit stove. 'This is my vice, Sister Carrol. I am hopelessly addicted to tea.'

'Please call me Eve.' She accepted a china cup of steaming green tea, and sipped it gratefully. It was refreshing and revitalising.

'Eve.' Lisa said it with a slight accent. 'The first woman in the Garden of Eden—am I right?' She handed a cup to Dr Craig.

He said, his voice harsh, 'You'll find the jungle around here is no Garden of Eden. One thing I must make clear. Stay within the hospital precincts, particularly at night.'

The rosy glow that had begun to surround Eve vanished like a pricked soap bubble. The gunfire . . . Her fear and suspicions came flooding back. She turned to Andrew Craig, setting down her cup, so that she could question him more fully. But Lisa intercepted with a gentle reprimand. 'Oh, Dr Craig, what an introduction! We'll have dinner first, and tell Eve the good things about Dantang, as well as the bad.'

'I won't stay for dinner, Lisa. I promised the Sultan I'd see him this evening, and I'll have dinner with them.'

Eve tried not to be impressed by his casual name-dropping. With scarcely a flicker of an eyelid, she picked up her tea and sipped it.

'Very well, Doctor. You will be here in the morning, though?'

'I'll be here.' Eve noticed a look between them—not an intimate look, but one of understanding and appreciation. They were old friends, that was clear. She realised they must have worked together for some time, the graceful oriental lady and the dashingly handsome man . . . Eve allowed her gaze to dwell on Andrew Craig a little longer. When his eyes were gentle, as they were now, she thought it possible that he was the best looking man she had ever met. In all her years of nursing, Eve realised she had never thought that of any of the distinguished and interesting doctors she had worked with.

Then, suddenly, she realised Craig had turned and had caught her staring at him. She put her cup down on the small table, to hide a fierce blush. 'I must wash. I must look like some sort of pathetic orphan.'

'That's right.' Andrew Craig's voice was steely again. He had clearly not been impressed by his first meeting with the new Sister. Eve clenched her jaw. She would make him revise that opinion when he saw how hard she meant to work. Not that it mattered to her—he was a rude and blunt man, and Eve had no time for men with no manners.

There was a savoury smell of cooking drifting in the smooth warm air. After being in Malaysia for the past five years, Eve was quick to recognise the familiar spices—the nutmeg, ginger, garlic, the coconut milk. Lisa noticed her interest. 'I must introduce you to Anya. She is a wonderful cook, and she looks after us all so well. Doctor, are you sure you will not stay?'

Craig rose, unfolding lithe limbs and stretching his back, so that it was impossible not to see how athletic and fit he was, and how perfectly his clothes were made. The muscles in his thighs strained against the cool cloth as he apologised for having to leave—but not to Eve. 'I'd like to, but the Palace is expecting me.' He strode across the metal bridge to his car, leaving the muslin curtain swinging, with hardly a nod of farewell. Lisa ignored his manners. She must be used to him by now.

'Come,' she said, 'I think a shower must be the only thing in the world you want at this moment.' And as the drone of Dr Craig's engine faded into the alert animal world of the jungle, Eve agreed wholeheartedly. Lisa led the way along a corridor. 'The main ward is downstairs at the back. All our personal rooms are on the first floor. I like to keep the front room as ours. It means we have a pleasant view in the day-time, and also that we are readily available if anyone needs us urgently from the village, or if the telephone rings.'

Eve had left her muddy sandals at the door, in the usual oriental custom. Now they ascended a bare wooden staircase, which felt blessedly cool to her feet.

'This will be your room.' It was small and white, and smelled clean and slightly antiseptic. There was a single bed, a wardrobe, and a dressing-table and mirror, with a smaller table in the corner holding a bookcase. To Eve's relief, there was a small additional fan on the dressing-table, rotating with a whirr as welcome as music. Lisa went to the window. There was no glass, and the ornamental grille was wound round with scented creepers from the outside wall.

'The bathroom is across the yard.' She pointed to a stone building across a paved yard, where grass and flowers sprang up between the flags, and crickets sang all around them. 'But there is a small hand-basin and toilet just down the corridor.' Lisa left Eve to refresh herself.

The shower was a small, concrete-floored room with a nozzle in the roof. The water flowed away down a hole in the floor. Eve revelled in the cool droplets, happy to be here. Dantang seemed to offer so much more than the luxury of the private hospital in Kuala Lumpur. As she shook the water from her hair and wrapped herself in her cotton robe, she realised just how bored she had been with her elegant flat in the nurses' home in KL. Here in

Dantang, she would find out just how good a nurse she was. The people were poor. They did not demand attention, as she had been used to. And she knew she and Lisa would be working unsupervised. It was a challenge and a thrill to have this chance.

Back in her little white room, Eve breathed in the cleanliness of it, the antiseptic combined with the sweetness of the creeper at the window. There was a sudden hard scutter of claws. Eve looked up with a smile at the family of apple-green lizards on the ceiling. The Malays believed that having these lizards in the house brought luck. They must be a fortunate race, for the lizards bred everywhere, except the luxury hotels and elegant houses where the people were sophisticated and westernised.

The lizards changed position again and then stood stock still, as though posing. Eve smiled. Dantang was where she wanted to be.

CHAPTER TWO

Eve lifted her suitcase on to the bed, and unlocked it. 'Oh, no!' She had brought the wrong one. This one contained her underclothes, her nightwear, her towels and toiletries. She lifted the carefully packed things feverishly. Surely there must be one dress? But no. Not even a Sister's navy blue uniform dress.

There was a tap on the door. 'Is everything all right, Eve?' Lisa came into the room. 'Food is ready.'

Eve ruefully explained her predicament. 'Lucky I had my bathrobe in my shoulder-bag.'

'That is no problem. I will lend you some clothes until tomorrow.' And Lisa was soon back from her own room with two batik sarongs, with two matching blouses. 'I think we must be about the same size. Please take these. There is no hurry to return them.' She shook one out. 'You know how to put on the sarong? It fastens at the waist—here—and the folds are at the front, so that you can walk without falling over.'

Eve tucked the soft cotton material into the waistband and surveyed her image in the mirror. 'How very flattering.' She had chosen a cloth in shades of pale mauve, blue and pink, which set off her fair colouring. The blouse to match was in delicate blue. Eve brushed her hair, dry now after her shower, and it curled fetchingly down to her shoulders and showed off the bare neck, where the skin was tanned a soft honey colour.

Lisa, after laughing at her attempts to get it right, now looked approving. 'It does suit you. You must buy some of your own.'

'Perhaps I will. But I'm here to work, not to play. Tell me about the hospital, Lisa.' They went downstairs together, where they found the table laid with a banquet of curries, fresh vegetables and fruit, and a pile of savoury pancakes. Eve had forgotten how hungry she was. And they both did full justice to Anya's cooking.

'She is a marvellous woman. She is from the village, and she comes here every day. She helps in the ward when we are busy, and stays away when she knows we are okay. You will find her always at your elbow when you need her most. You can rely on her when I am not here.'

'You mean—you aren't staying on?' Eve looked across at her new friend, who was calmly helping herself to more fried rice with capsicums and cashew nuts. 'Just when I thought we would be working together?'

Lisa smiled as she took a dainty mouthful. 'I am due for leave. But not until you know the ropes. And of course, Dr Craig is only a telephone call away.'

'Dr Craig.' Eve's voice implied that she would not be calling him.

'He always leaves a telephone number. You know he has three other village hospitals to look after?'

'He told me.' She quietly hoped he would find business at the other three more pressing. Dr Craig might be a good doctor, but she doubted that he would be good as a friend and companion. 'Any other help?'

Lisa passed over a dish of tender lamb kebabs. 'Yes, Zaina from the village. She's a trained auxiliary. She will stay all night if you need her. I usually let her go home. She has a husband and a young child, and it is better that she stay with them.'

'Of course.'

Later that night, Eve lay on the bed, covered only by a thin cotton sheet, and looked up at the lizards in the moonlight, their shadows long and exaggerated on the white ceiling. She had been sleepy earlier, but now, stimulated by the prospect of working here, she felt alive and vibrant. What a challenge. She knew it could be a good life here. Even if Lisa went on leave, she could cope with Zaina and Anya to help. She would be answerable only to Andrew Craig. And she would soon demonstrate to him that his presence was not necessary in Dantang.

Eve listened to the sounds of the jungle. Already she was used to them. They were no longer menacing—just natural, just there, along with the moonlight and the sweet-smelling creeper at the window grille. Sleep began to make her eyelids heavy. Her eyes closed and the crickets' chorus hummed into the distance as sleep came. Then, almost as unconsciousness overtook her, there came the purr of a certain dark green Rover, and she heard someone walking over the bridge over the monsoon drain. She heard a key in the lock . . .

Then she was suddenly wide awake. There came a single long whistle, like the one she had heard at the garage that evening. After the shots. It came from the trees. And she heard someone gently close the front door again, and walk back across the bridge. Curiosity forced her to the window. She trembled with excitement as she brushed back tousled curls from her face and peered through the iron grille at the shadowy jungle.

The moon was brilliant, an orange orb slung low and large over the trees. Andrew Craig was standing at the very edge of the jungle, one long leg relaxed, leaning like some fashion-plate against a palm trunk. Even at this time of night he did not look ruffled, nor tired. Only his black hair was slightly out of place, a curl like a question mark hanging over his tanned forehead.

Then Eve gasped aloud. Out of the jungle appeared a

slim figure. He wore a soldier's uniform, jacket and trousers in camouflage print, a peaked baseball-type cap pulled down over the broad Malay face. He leaned towards the doctor, and the two heads were close together as some words were exchanged. Then Dr Craig took something out of his pocket. The man accepted it, and melted into the jungle. Craig straightened up and walked with measured steps back to the front door.

Eve's trembling had gone. Just as in Casualty, when she was always able to control her initial feelings of panic and take control of whatever cases she had to deal with, so now she became very calm and cool. She wondered if she should go down, make it clear that she had seen him? Then she thought again of that long, low whistle. It was a secret. A secret Dr Craig might not wish to share with his staff. Eve went back to bed and closed her eyes. Her heart was thumping as she heard him mount the stairs to his room. But in a very few moments her natural weariness had sent her into a deep sleep . . .

In the morning, the event seemed as though it had been part of a dream. Eve was eager to start work in her jungle hospital. She washed hurriedly and dressed in the pastel coloured sarong she had worn the previous night. It was a strange uniform to start her new duties in, but she would go down to Abbas's later to collect her other case. She breathed in the fresh morning air, laden with forest scents and sounds. What a change from the busy traffic of a Monday morning in KL.

'Good morning, Eve. You slept well?' Lisa was already sitting at the table, sipping freshly-squeezed orange juice and eating toast and marmalade. 'Anya will cook eggs for you if you wish it.'

Eve shook her head. She sat down and helped herself to a couple of tiny bananas and a slice of toast. 'These are fresh from the garden?' Lisa nodded, and indicated the front of the hospital. Eve smiled a contented smile. 'I shall feel as though I am on holiday every single morning I am working here.' The birds sang lustily outside, and Eve heard what sounded like running water. 'Is there a river near here?'

Lisa's face darkened slightly. 'There is a stream. But we do not go into the jungle alone.'

Eve poured coffee from a glass jug. 'But why? It must be near enough to shout for help if you fall in?'

Lisa said quickly, 'Do not underestimate the jungle. Once inside, it is impossible to find your way out. Believe me. And there are many snakes and insects with poisonous bites. We have a fridge in the dispensary with many remedies for these things. I will show you. Many of them can be fatal.'

Eve nodded. 'Don't worry. I'll remember.' She sipped the fragrant coffee. That soldier she had seen last night had not seemed worried by snakes and creepy-crawlies. She said casually, 'Did Dr Craig come back last night?'

'I do not know. My room is at the back.' The Malay girl's almond eyes were alert and wide, yet Eve wondered if she was hiding anything. Lisa called out, 'Anya?'

Anya was small, middle-aged and alert. She wore a dark brown sarong with a black, short-sleeved blouse. She had the manner of a tiny bird, making quick, darting movements. 'Is the doctor back, Anya?'

'Oh yes, Missy Kai. See—his car is in the grass.' She bent her head towards Eve. '*Salaam*, Missy Carrol. I hope that you like stay here.' And Eve won a smile from the wary little face, when she praised the meal of the night before.

'Well, do I see the ward now?' Eve was eager to start. Anya began clearing the table.

Lisa laughed. 'There is no hurry here, Eve.'

'But the patients? Don't they get breakfast?' It seemed all wrong for the nurses to eat first.

Lisa shook her head. 'Anya has given them breakfast. But we have no set routine, as you do in the cities. Very often the families of the patients bring them food themselves. And we only have two in-patients just now.'

'Two?'

'One is very ill, and not expected to live. We keep him comfortable. The other is a child—a girl with a chest infection. I kept her in so that Dr Craig can see her today.'

They went along the cool corridor towards the ward. It was clean and smelt of the same antiseptic that pervaded the hospital. The six beds were simple and functional, with screens that could be pulled round at will. The girl with suspected pneumonia was about seven, and she lay listlessly in the corner bed.

Eve smiled down at her. 'How are you?' She spoke in Malay. 'I'm Sister Carrol.' She bent and took the child's pulse. The girl smiled weakly, but said nothing. Eve said to Lisa, 'Shall I change her sheets?'

'Zaina will be in to do that soon.' Lisa bent to the child. 'I have told the nice doctor and he will come and make you well very soon.'

Lisa was ready to leave the ward. Eve pointed to the other corner. 'Tell me about him.' All they could see was a brown face against the white pillow. The man was so thin that he hardly made a hump under the thin white coverlet. 'Is it cancer?'

'Old Jacko? No, nothing like that. He has brought it upon himself. He is an alcoholic—drunk himself to death. Liver failure.'

Eve stared at the still figure. 'Poor man.'

'Not really,' Lisa said. 'At least he is comfortable

here. He doesn't have to lie in a dirty shack waiting for his end.'

'Why not transfer him to the hospital in Jahin? You said all serious cases went there.'

Lisa led Eve to the small niche at the end of the ward, where, behind a sheet of glass, they could look through yet not be overheard.

'Eve, again you are talking like a city girl. Life here is different. Jacko is alcoholic. Nobody wants him, nobody cares about him. He has no home. If we sent him to Jahin they would only send him back to make room for some cases that are treatable.'

'Where did he get drink?'

'Have you not heard of palm wine? The peasants can always find it if they want it. No, Eve, Jacko wants to die. And we understand his wish, and leave him to die with dignity, not with tubes all over him and no rest. See how peaceful he is.'

'May I give him some tea?'

Lisa shrugged. 'If you wish.' She rose. 'I will be starting the clinic in a moment—outside the hospital. I have asked several patients to come up this morning to be examined by Dr Craig.'

'Very well.' Eve walked back to old Jacko's bedside. His wrinkled face was peaceful, no doubt, but it went against her training to allow someone to die, however humane it seemed. She stood for a while, staring down at him. He was her patient now, her responsibility. She bent over the inert shape. 'Good morning, Jacko.'

There was no response from the recumbent figure. Had she really expected a miracle? She stood at the foot of his bed, her head bent in pity and regret. She did not see that she was being watched as she wrestled with her conscience. Surely it could not be right just to leave poor

Jacko here? Comfortable or not, it was her duty to save his life, not leave him.

'Sister Carrol.'

Eve spun round at the dark brown voice. 'Good morning, Dr Craig.'

'Is that a suitable uniform, do you think?' Craig's face was impassive, the black eyebrows making him look stern. She noticed that in daylight his eyes were a clear blue, not black, as they had seemed when seen in the shadows of the night before. Eve looked down at her graceful sarong, too astonished at his rudeness to reply. She had forgotten she was wearing it. The doctor came towards her into the ward. 'You are not on holiday, you know. You look as though you are going to a party. Please go and change.'

Eve was used to thinking quickly. She had discovered long ago that some men used disapproval to make themselves feel more important. She had no intention of letting Andrew Craig make her feel small ever again. She straightened her shoulders and looked the physician directly in the eye. She totally ignored the glowering look he gave to her pastel sarong, to the thin muslin blouse, low-necked, with its tiny pearl buttons and small sleeves that showed off slim arms.

'I am glad you are here, Doctor. What do you think of this patient? I wonder if I ought to transfer him to Jahin as an emergency?' Her voice was very firm and businesslike. Her chin came up, and she smiled sweetly, as she saw he was taken aback by her attitude.

He forced his eyes back to poor Jacko. 'Sister Kai made it clear that this man's liver damage must be totally irreversible by now. He has no chance of a useful life, Sister.' He sighed and turned away from the poor fellow. 'In the interest of humanity, Sister Carrol, it's sometimes kinder not to interfere too much with nature.'

'I know that,' Eve said with some emotion. 'But who is to decide when that time has come?'

Andrew Craig looked gravely down at his new assistant, and his face was far from tranquil. His voice was even less so. 'Sister, you are not in charge here. You know that in medicine it is sometimes necessary to obey a decision not completely your own. I suggest you go and change into a more suitable uniform. We will discuss this patient at a later date, when Sister Kai can also be present.' He stood, one leg relaxed, as she had seen him the previous night, standing against the tree. But his angry eyes belied the easy stance, as they glared down on his assistant, expecting Eve to quail beneath their impact.

He turned towards the door and took a stethoscope from his pocket. 'I will be at the clinic. Please come along as soon as you have changed.'

She stamped after him, unable to hide her irritation. 'My uniform is in the van at Abbas's. Isn't it better that I watch how things are done here, rather than trail down there while you are here to teach me?'

He turned his back on her completely, forging ahead of her. It wasn't the first time a doctor had done that, either. She knew very well that some of them regarded themselves as too high up for criticism. Andrew Craig was showing all the signs of being in this category. 'Oh, come on, then, woman. There's work to be done.' The tetchy comment confirmed Dr Craig in Eve's mind as one of the least agreeable colleagues she had ever worked with. When he spoke like that, she could hear a hint of a Scottish accent in his voice. But she banished visions of a cosy cottage childhood. This man must have been a pest of a child, to have such an ego. She remembered one of her friends describing a man of this type as being 'quarried, not born', and it was with a secret smile that she followed her chief out into the glorious morning sunshine.

Lisa and Zaina had taken out tables, a couple of chairs and boxes of medicines and dressings. There was a pad on which to make notes, a sphygmomanometer and an auroscope. Craig sat at one of the tables, Lisa at another. Eve stood behind Craig, only to be told irritably to bring another chair. She smiled again as she obeyed sweetly, knowing it made him more cross.

There were three women squatting patiently, waiting in the shadow of the trees beyond the car park, two with small children. Craig beckoned with one finger, and the first one approached with the simple grace of the Malay, her bare feet treading the dry grass delicately. 'Sister Kai say you want to see me. My daughter, Suky, she is in the hospital.'

'Ah, yes, good. Come along. We'll take another look at her chest and see whether she needs to stay in or not.' Craig's voice was no longer tetchy. It was like dark honey, inspiring confidence in a woman worried about her child. As they went, he demanded the case history from Lisa.

'Would you be good enough to see the next patient for me, Sister?' he asked Eve.

Somewhat surprised at his unexpected courtesy, Eve returned to her chair and smiled at the next woman in the queue. It was a simple case. The baby had an abrasion on its little face, which was turning a little septic. Eve washed it gently in antiseptic lotion, admiring its sweet expression as she did so, to the mother's pleasure. 'Just keep it clean and dry until it heals.' She gave her some cream, and put a dry dressing over the lesion.

'Thank you, okay, I do. When I come for next injection in arm?'

Eve rifled through Lisa's list of children and found the patient's name. She checked the date of the last inoculation and gave her a card with the date the next was due.

The next woman was concerned because her child was very small. Again, Eve checked the records, finding that she had been a small baby, and indeed, was gaining weight at quite a satisfactory rate. Eve was able to reassure her, in a mixture of Malay and English, that not all healthy babies had to be fat. 'Your daughter is going to be small and dainty, like you,' she said, and smiled at the anxiety of the first-time mother—the same in any country.

There was more of a queue forming now. Eve saw a couple more before Dr Craig came back. She removed some stitches from a youth's cut hand, and she was able to get a nasty splinter of wood from a girl's arm. She was just giving an anti-tetanus injection, when he arrived to take over.

'You seem to have managed.'

'There has been nothing difficult, Doctor. But I think there's someone waiting to see you.'

'Right. Thanks, I'll take over. But may I just warn you—you might see nothing but trivia all morning. Never let it blind you into security. We must always be alert for the serious case. These people do not complain. You must be aware there might be something serious, and always question them well.' He sat down, and looked at the brief notes Eve had made. 'Well done.' He beckoned the next patient, a woman clearly in pain.

Eve had no time to savour the compliment as she saw the way the woman clutched at her stomach. Lisa said urgently, 'This lady had pain yesterday, Doctor. Not so bad. I thought it was a pelvic infection.'

'Did you start her on antibiotics?'

'Yes, sir.' Lisa was helping the woman up the steps. Eve did not wait to be asked. Zaina and Lisa assisted the doctor, while Eve got on with the lesser problems of the village people.

Lisa came down the steps. 'Dr Craig thinks she has a tubal pregnancy. I will just go and find someone who can take her to Jahin.'

'What happens if there is no one?'

'Then you or I must take her. Or we telephone for the ambulance to come from Jahin.' Lisa ran across to the waiting villagers, and one of them apparently volunteered to run down to the village for the woman's husband.

Dr Craig came out. 'Sister Carrol, would you stay with her? She's in a lot of pain and there's some bleeding. Check her temperature, and make a note of how often she gets these cramps in her pelvis.' Eve ran up the steps to the ward and washed her hands before sitting by the bedside of the sick woman.

The child in the corner coughed. Eve said, 'You want some water, Suky?' She poured a drink for the child, using cold water from a bottle in the fridge. As she passed the bed where old Jacko lay, she heard a low moan. She gave Suky the water and made sure the woman was comfortable, then she hurried back to Jacko. 'Are you all right? *Baiklah*, Jacko?'

Eve waited, hearing her own heartbeats in the quiet room. The man in the bed stirred and opened his eyes. She bent down. 'Is it water?' She moistened the dry lips and saw the dark eyes focus on her face, then become more animated. She was suddenly rewarded by a broad smile, showing several teeth missing. It was not a pretty smile—but to Eve it was as joyful as someone coming back from the dead. She patted the thin shoulder and administered more water from a cup with a spout.

There was a shrill scream from the woman in the other bed and Eve ran across. She was clutching her stomach and groaning. Tears poured from her eyes, down the smooth dark cheeks. 'Ram, oh, Ram!'

Lisa had hurried in. She took the woman's hand firmly. 'Your husband is on his way.' She spoke in Malay. Zaina, a young, plump girl with curly black hair tied in a bushy tail down her back, came round the other side of the bed. She lifted the sheet. The woman was bleeding again. It was partly the shame of this that was upsetting her.

'Do you keep plasma here?'

'A couple of bottles only.'

'Then wouldn't it be better to get the ambulance? They will have supplies.'

Lisa showed a certain impatience. 'Don't try to take charge on the first day. Only last week I dealt with a ruptured appendix my way. And the telephone was out of order.'

Eve was appalled. 'What happened?'

'He made it. I drove him to Kuanang and called the hospital from there. The ambulance met me, and the patient was in theatre within thirty-five minutes.'

'He must have been lucky.' Eve was amazed at the casual way Lisa spoke of her emergencies.

Lisa nodded. 'Lucky that he came to Lisa,' Zaina said. 'The Bomoh told him he had eaten poisoned meat.'

'The Bomoh?'

Andrew Craig was suddenly there, and they stood aside as he felt the woman's pulse and took her blood pressure. He watched the mercury in the sphig falling gently, and listened to the throb of the blood in her arm. 'The Bomoh is the local medicine man. Steer clear of him. He doesn't trust us. And he certainly doesn't like the way we keep making people better.'

'Medicine man? You mean—as in witch doctor?'

'I do, Sister. And if there are no patients waiting, then I suggest you pop down to the gas station before lunch and pick up your van. Then perhaps you could get some decent clothes on.'

Eve stared, her blue eyes angry. She had thought he was beginning to be pleasant for one moment out there in the sunshine. He took no notice. She turned, after looking carefully at what the other two nurses were wearing. Lisa wore a pale batik top over white trousers. Zaina wore a sarong. Why pick on her? Why should she in a sarong be improperly dressed, while the other two were not?

She walked down the steps of the veranda into the sunshine. There was a small stout woman waiting by the desk, holding the arm of a sheepish teenage boy. 'You the doctor?' She dragged the boy, who looked the picture of glowing good health, with bright eyes, and firm, rounded muscles, and stood him before Eve.

'I'm the new Sister here. What is the trouble?'

'Mat, my son. He have such great pain in the night.' The boy shuffled his feet as his mother told the tale. Eve turned to the boy.

He nodded. 'Yes, I have pain. Here, in my shoulder at the back.' He tried to point round his own back. The joint appeared to move quite freely now. 'I could not sleep until I sat up with lot of pillows.'

'And is the pain still there?'

'No pain now. Everything okay, *lah*.' He swung his arm, just to demonstrate, and looked down at his anxious mother, showing her that she had embarrassed him. Eve prodded the joint, and moved it for herself. There was no reaction from the boy.

'Well, it seems fine now. Did you bang it at all, or did the pain come on unexpectedly?'

'No, no bang it.'

His mother interrupted. 'Those boys, they always playing rough. They do kung fu after school.'

'Kung fu? Then perhaps the joint was dislocated a little when you were fighting, and now it has slipped back into place. Stay and have a word with Dr Craig. He won't be a moment.'

The woman smiled broadly. Eve had given her a good enough explanation of Mat's pain and she was satisfied. 'No need. This boy, he better get back to school, lah.'

They walked off down the dirt road. They passed a battered little Honda car, rattling up the track, and the husband of the sick woman jumped out, his face drawn with anxiety. Lisa and Andrew Craig together carried the woman to the car and settled her in the back seat, while Eve was sent to telephone the hospital at Jahin. 'Yes, she may need blood. No, there is no need for the ambulance. Her husband is bringing her. Should be there in about forty minutes. Yes, a gynae emergency.'

She came out again. The little Honda was already on the way, and Lisa and Dr Craig were sitting calmly in the sunshine. Andrew Craig tipped his chair back on two legs and looked Eve deliberately up and down. She had completely forgotten about her dress, but this reminded her, and she smoothed the sarong nervously over her neat hips at his appraisal. 'Well, if you can't obey me about your dress, how about making some coffee, Sister?'

She refused to be annoyed. 'Of course. I don't know any nurses who can't do that. And then would you talk over some of the patients with me? I'd like to know what you decided about Suky. And can I have your permission to give Jacko a little more mental stimulation?'

Dr Craig's eyes, now quite a piercing blue in the full daylight, widened in surprise at her polite refusal to be

bullied. Then, with a weary gesture that was only half in
fun, he pulled the morning's notes towards him. 'I knew
I should have appointed an oriental Sister. They know
how to pamper a tired, thirsty physician.' He picked out
Suky's file. But before he could say any more, Anya
appeared with a tray, on which were four cups and a pot
of fragrant coffee. Eve hid a smile, and Andrew Craig
pretended not to notice.

'Yes, Suky can go home when her temperature has
been stable for twenty-four hours.'

Eve was tempted to mention Jacko again, but it was
her first day and Lisa and Dr Craig had already made
their position clear. She was wise enough to realise she
must tread warily for the first few days at least, until she
knew more about the hospital. Dr Craig pushed away his
empty cup. 'I'll be off, then. I'll be at the Palace for
lunch, and then back at the Jahin office for the night.
You have both phone numbers? Fine.'

He brushed the hibiscus petals from the roof of his car
and drove away into the deep shadows of the shimmering midday jungle. The three nurses went indoors for a
sandwich lunch, and then to their rooms, to sleep to the
gentle whirr of the fans and the scuttle of lizards on the
walls.

Eve was first to wake. The afternoon was still and
sleepy. She showered and put on the other sarong Lisa
had lent her, a pretty combination of green and gold. I
must go down to the village for my things, she thought,
but she did not go immediately. She wandered out of the
front door, listening with pleasure to the drowsy noises
of the jungle, the buzz of bees, the occasional subdued
squawk of the vivid macaws that swooped from the trees
above her. She crossed the monsoon drain and walked
across the clearing towards the enticing scented gloom
that was the forest.

'*Jangan sekali-kali masuk seaorang ke dalam hutan!*' Lisa's warning was shrill. 'Don't go in there alone, Eve! I have warned you. Promise me you won't be so reckless.'

Startled by the vehemence of Lisa's voice, Eve came back and joined her on the veranda. '*Baiklah*, Lisa, *baiklah*. All right, I won't. I am going down to the gas station for my things in a moment.'

Lisa calmed down. 'Sorry, but it is dangerous.'

'Everything looks so harmless. Whatever Dr Craig said, it does remind me of the Garden of Eden. You have lovely weather, a tinkling little stream, no man-eating tigers, and a garden full of fruits and vegetables!'

Lisa nodded. 'I know you are going to like it here. But it has its dark side. Trust me. It is not always so idyllic.'

Eve grinned. 'Especially when Attila the Hun is around.'

'Who?'

'Dr Andrew Craig. How long have you known him? Where does he learn his excellent manners?'

'You are sarcastic.' Lisa was not used to irony.

'Well, tell me something about him.'

'He is very kind, very good,' Zaina said.

Lisa agreed, but Eve noticed that she was not meeting her gaze. Those almond eyes were hooded, and she spoke with that typical impassiveness that Eve had got used to since living in Malaysia. Eve envied this skill. She always showed her feelings, with a sometimes embarrassing spontaneity. Lisa went on, 'Well, he is a single man. He is, I think, a man who does not need others. He is always alone.'

'No friends?' Eve was not entirely surprised, if he spoke to everyone as he had to her. 'Surely he relaxes sometimes?'

'He visits the Sultan a lot. The Sultana is ill, but he also visits as a friend, I think. He was at university with the

Sultan in Cambridge. The chief surgeon in Jahin was also one of his colleagues. That is what brought him here to Malaysia. And he has never left. He has been in this present post for seven years.'

'And always alone?' Eve imagined him, striding alone through life, surrounded by beauty, yet not happy. 'Poor man.'

CHAPTER THREE

THEY sat in the late afternoon sun under the shade of the veranda, watching the shadows lengthen, talking fitfully about life and what they had done before they came to Dantang. Eve did not mention Andrew Craig again. She recognised that he and Lisa had a long association with the hospital, and that Lisa was a loyal and discreet colleague.

'You know that Jacko opened his eyes today? He took some water, and smiled. He can't be so near death, Lisa.' They were drinking Lisa's favourite green tea, so cooling and welcome in the heat. 'I bet he'd like some tea.'

'Very well.' Lisa signalled with one dainty wrist, and Zaina poured some tea and took it indoors. 'You see, I am not heartless, Eve. Only very realistic. I have been here a long time.'

There was a distant noise of laughter, rising above the chirping and whistling of the birds in the trees above them. Eve sat up.

'It is the women in the plantation having a joke. They must be working on the trees at this side of the plantation,' Lisa said.

'The women? Where are the men?'

'They work in the fields, care for their own animals and grow their own crops. Collecting the latex from the rubber trees is light work, only for the women.'

Eve leaned back against the wooden strut that supported the sloping roof, and lifted her face to catch the hint of warm wind. As she did so, she heard a familiar sound, the rattling engine of her van. She stood up. Yes. Driven by the redoubtable Abbas, her van was riding the slope.

'I bring van, Missy Carrol. All filled up good. You not mad at me now, uh?' He parked the van in the shade of the jungle trees.

She could not be angry with him. He had saved her a journey. 'Thank you. What do I owe you, Abbas?' She walked across the metal bridge to collect her luggage.

'Okay, *baiklah*. You pay any time. I write in the book your name.'

That suited Eve and she nodded as he mopped his brow before turning to walk down to his garage, his plump behind swaying in the old check sarong. Eve opened the van door. 'My case—it's missing!' She climbed in and rifled feverishly under cushions and rugs. 'It isn't here!' she protested.

'No, Missy Carrol. No one go near that van. I fill with gas when delivery truck come, and bring straight to you. Key is there,' Abbas insisted after she had called him back.

'It's all right. I'm not blaming you,' Eve placated him.

Lisa said, 'I would swear that the village people wouldn't touch it. What was in it?'

'My best clothes. About ten dresses, and two changes of uniform.' Eve looked rueful. 'I suppose it could have been worse. But I can't go on wearing your clothes. You'll need them when you go on leave.' And with a grin, she said, 'And Attila the Hun won't be too pleased either!'

But it was too warm to be worried, and they sat with a jug of fresh lime juice Anya had decided they needed. Eve leaned back, totally comfortable. She arched her spine and stretched her limbs like a cat. As she put her arms down again, she remembered young Mat and the pain in his shoulder. The shoulder that only hurt him when he lay down . . .

'Oh yes, of course!' She almost shouted the words, startling a flock of Indian starlings, who took off with a rattle of wing-feathers. 'Oh, God, Lisa, I sent him away! What a fool I am!' Eve jumped to her feet. 'Lisa, I've done something dreadful.'

'What, what?' Lisa stood up also, dark eyes worried, forehead puckered in alarm.

'The boy, Mat—you weren't there, but I saw him. He'd had a shoulder pain. I must find him at once. Get in the van!'

As she drove, Eve explained. 'Referred pain. I saw one once in London, a rugby player who only had pain when he lay down.'

'And where was the pain referred from?'

'Spleen, Lisa—ruptured spleen. Oh God, I hope I'm wrong. He'd have no pain until the leaking blood touches a nerve. Oh, why didn't I get Dr Craig to see him?'

They had reached a clearing, on the outskirts of the village. Eve had no eyes for the quaint wooden houses with carved roof ends, nestling between banana trees and mangoes. She jumped out. 'Where will he be?'

Lisa asked a couple of startled villagers. 'The boy who came to hospital this morning, the big boy? Find him please.'

In a few minutes, the mother was found. 'He is at school, Sister. He felt very well.'

They ran back to the van. Lisa was pointing further up the road. 'There, that is the school, among the trees. You drive up. I will phone the Palace and tell Dr Craig. We will have to get him to Jahin.'

Eve felt her chest ache with tension as she drove into the school grounds. She jumped out, calling as she went:

'*Salaam*, I am Sister from the hospital. Where is Mat Abdullah?'

A bewildered Tamil lady in a pale blue sari came to the entrance. Eve began to tell her tale, and the teacher soon realised the gravity of the situation. 'Yes, Mat Abdullah. He missed morning school. I think he is in the lab.' She led the way, her sari floating in the breeze, to another prefabricated building where test tubes and retort stands were visible through the windows. Mat was there.

He looked strong, sturdy. 'Yes, miss?'

'Mat, this is important. Did you have a fall yesterday? Any kind of fall?'

The broad face creased in a smile of amazement that she should know. 'Yes, miss. I was doing kung fu with Encik Beli, and I fell into the monsoon drain. I was not hurt. The drain was empty.'

'You must come with me, Mat.' Eve tried to keep her voice very calm. 'I want you to see the doctor about that fall. Just a precaution.'

'Am I ill, miss?' They were already driving down the road. Eve had paused only to speak to Lisa, who was standing at the roadside, and they were well on the way before she realised she had not even stopped to put her sandals on.

'You may have a bit of internal injury, Mat. I just want a second opinion, that's all.' Lisa had not been able to find Andrew Craig. There was nothing for it but to get the boy to Jahin Hospital as soon as possible.

'Will I be all right?'

'Of course. I'm just taking no chances, okay?'

Jahin was a small town, busy with late shoppers, bicycles and trishaws in the narrow streets. Thank goodness the way to the hospital was clearly signposted. It was only half an hour later that Eve was drawing up in a parking place marked *Ambulan*, and there at the door was a porter with a trolley, and a nurse, waiting for them.

The porter looked sceptically at the big, healthy boy and Eve began to have doubts herself. Wiping the sweat from her face and neck with her handkerchief, she said quickly, 'He had better not lie down, thank you. Can we see the surgeon, please?' Her manner was cool, but inside she felt nervous. They would laugh at her, in her sarong and bare feet, her untidy hair, her hot, streaked face. The sister who drove all the way from Dantang with a healthy boy . . .

The porter shrugged and went off with the trolley. The small student nurse said, 'Mr Dalasingam is along here.' She led them along a corridor into a small consulting room with a large window, covered now with a venetian blind, for evening was falling fast.

The dapper little Indian rose from his desk. 'Now, Sister, what is all this?'

Mat stepped forward hesitantly. Eve said quickly, 'Sir, my name is Sister Eve Carrol. I know I may be wrong, but this boy fell heavily yesterday. Today he complained of pain in his shoulder . . .'

The consultant looked mildly annoyed, and interrupted, 'Then surely you need the orthopods, Sister?'

Eve swallowed hard. 'I'd be grateful if you would look at him, sir. I think he may have ruptured his spleen.'

There was a sudden change in the surgeon's manner, and he motioned the boy over to the examination couch. Within minutes, Mat Abdullah was whisked off to the theatre. Eve sat in the empty consulting room, forgotten, but very relieved to have been proved right. She was too weary now to feel elated. There was just a numb feeling of thankfulness that she had been in time.

The door was pushed open and someone came in and

turned on a small table lamp. Eve blinked in the unexpected light and looked up, pushing back a limp lock
of hair. He spoke, and his voice was dark brown and
cool. 'So, Sister Carrol is still in fancy dress.'

'Dr Craig!' He had the power to annoy her in very few
words. She sat up straight and looked into the darkly
handsome face. There he stood, bandbox smart as ever.
He made her realise just how crumpled and travel-
stained she must be, her feet dirty with rushing through
the grass at the school. He sat down in the consultant's
chair and rested one elegant hand on the desk, drum-
ming the fingers softly as he stared across at her.

'That was a dramatic cross-country dash.' She
couldn't tell if he were praising or deriding her.

'A drama I could have done without.' She kept her
reply as brief as possible. She could hear a clock ticking
in the corridor and the hushed chatter of nurses as they
passed the half-open door.

'Shall I get you a cup of tea?'

She would have loved a cup of tea, but not with
Andrew Craig. 'No. I just want to hear that Mat is all
right. Then I'll phone the news to Lisa, and start back.'

'Very well.' He stood up. 'Don't forget to fill the tank
before you set off.' And he was gone from the room in a
couple of strides. Eve shook her head, puzzled no longer
at the curtness of the man. She moved her chair closer to
the desk so that she could rest her head on her arms, just
for a few moments . . .

She knew nothing more until she felt her shoulder
being gently shaken. Eve lifted her head from her arms,
wondering for a moment where she was. She rubbed her
eyes. 'Mat? How is he?'

The surgeon's voice was firm and reassuring. 'In
Recovery. He'll be fine. Well done, Sister Carrol. He
owes you his life.' Mr Dalasingam was still wearing his

green theatre gown and cap. His mask was pulled down round his neck. 'I knew you would want to be told.'

Eve shook her head to try and rid herself of the sudden weariness. She sat up straight and smiled broadly. Mat was all right. 'I must phone Lisa.' A warm feeling began to run through her body at the knowledge she had been right. She had saved a life. 'Can they get me Dantang Hospital? I can't remember the number.'

The surgeon picked up the telephone and quietly asked the switchboard. 'Sister Kai? Jahin Hospital here. Good news. Here is your colleague.' He handed the instrument to Eve.

'Lisa? Is Mrs Abdullah with you? Mat's going to be fine. Yes, splenectomy. Mr Dalasingam. He should be home in—' She looked up at the surgeon.

'Ten or twelve days.'

Eve repeated the news. 'I will be setting off soon, Lisa.'

Mr Dalasingam lifted a hand to interrupt her. 'You are dining with my wife and myself before you go. We cannot let you return without food and a rest.'

'I—' Eve could not refuse. 'That is very kind of you.' She ended her conversation with Lisa and replaced the phone. 'I'm not very respectable,' she said. 'I'm afraid I left Dantang rather hurriedly.'

'That is quite understandable.' He smiled. 'Having just saved a boy's life, you look very well indeed. You may tidy up at my house. I have told my wife to expect us.' He began to untie his mask. 'I will see you at the main door in five minutes, Sister Carrol.'

In a few minutes they were driving back along the leafy road by which she had entered the town. 'This is pretty. I didn't notice it earlier,' Eve commented.

Mr Dalasingam chuckled. 'I don't think I would either, if I were driving a ruptured spleen thirty miles through the jungle roads. That young lad's family owe you a lot.' He turned into a side-road, where clean white houses stood in their own neat green gardens. 'Here we are. And you are near the main highway for your return journey.'

They drew up at one of the white houses. Eve stared. There was her van, standing demurely outside. 'That—it *is* mine, isn't it?'

The surgeon smiled. 'I got a friend to bring it for you. And to fill the tank.'

'That's most awfully kind.' She wondered why he found it such a joke, until she saw the tall figure of Dr Craig, chatting at the door of the house to a very pretty Indian lady in a deep red sari. Of course. Lisa had told her that Andrew Craig was friendly with the chief surgeon. He turned round at that moment and his gaze was again coolly impersonal. 'Thank you very much, Dr Craig.'

'That's okay.' He didn't smile a lot, this man. She didn't know if he resented doing this favour for her, or whether he really was quite pleased that she had been able to save the boy's life. 'I am always grateful for a chance to eat Mrs Dalasingam's curry.'

They stood for a moment on the green lawn, chatting under the palm trees. Then her hostess said to Eve, 'I'm sure you would like to freshen up after your adventure. Do come along with me.'

Eve was grateful for her thoughtfulness. 'I did leave in quite a hurry.' She looked down at her grimy feet. 'Not fit to enter your lovely house.'

'There will be all you need in the bathroom.' The Indian woman led her inside and showed her where to go in the cool, tastefully decorated hall. 'We will be in the garden when you are ready.'

Eve took off her sarong and blouse, shook them well

and hung them up while she showered and rubbed her whole body with scented soap. How good it felt! When she was thoroughly clean and refreshed, she dressed again in the green and gold batik sarong, and smiled at her image in the full-length mirror. Andrew Craig disapproved. Yet it was only bad luck that she still had no chance of wearing anything else. Her slim form in the close-fitting sarong looked neat and attractive. The little blouse set off her tan, and the low neck allowed blonde tendrils of drying hair to curl down in the tropical heat over the brown skin. She had never bothered much with her appearance, but she knew she looked presentable.

Mrs Dalasingam had thoughtfully left a pair of Indian sandals for her. Slipping her toes into the narrow gold straps, Eve walked out to the garden, feeling good, and very satisfied with life. The crickets were giving their nightly serenade as she joined the other three at the rear of the house, where a small table bore four glasses, and bottles of Martini and fruit juices. The great moon had risen over the horizon and showed like some picture postcard between two fringed palm trees outlined in its light.

It was hard to believe she had only been in Selangor state for the last twenty-four hours. Eve sat back on the flower-decked patio and listened to the conversation. They were talking about their student days. She knew that Andrew Craig had only come out to Malaysia after learning of its charm and attraction from his friend. He explained to Eve, 'I did a student elective here. It was in paediatrics. It was enough to hook me for life, that four months.' Andrew Craig was getting his human look again, as he did with people he liked. And perhaps the Martini helped a little.

The meal was indeed a feast. They filled their plates

from a side table and brought them into the garden to eat. As well as a plate of steaming savoury rice, there were lentil curries, ladies' fingers and grilled cubes of meat, accompanied by large, freshly-made chapatis The conversation, and the wine, flowed freely, though Eve found that Andrew Craig tended to stay at the far end of the garden with his friend, leaving the two women together. Mrs Dalasingam, who insisted that Eve call her Mina, was delighted to have company, and they got on very well.

'I really don't want to go. But I must not leave Lisa alone any longer,' Eve said at last.

Her host and hostess came to the road to see her off. Dr Andrew Craig did not. Eve ignored his rudeness. Like Lisa Kai, she had come to terms with it. There were plenty of pleasant people in her life, so why let one man's lack of manners bother her?

Mina bent down, as Eve slipped into the driving seat and put the van into gear, and said, 'I do hope we meet again soon.' And Eve drove away with the memory of an evening that would stand out in her mind for many years—both for the kindness and hospitality of her hosts, and also the quiet and taciturn arrogance of the other guest.

She drove back under the attentive moon. The evening's meal and conversation had given her a warm glow, which was helped along by the gratified feeling that she had indeed saved young Mat's life. Mr Dalasingam had done the operation. But if Eve had not remembered that young rugby player in St Thomas's in London, seven years ago, then Mat might not be alive now.

The road to Dantang had not improved since last night and Eve found herself jolting and bouncing in the same muddy pot-holes she had got to know only yesterday. At least I won't run out of gas, she thought—thanks, surprisingly, to the thoughtfulness of Andrew Craig . . . Had she really called him Attila the Hun? Perhaps that was a little unnecessary.

With headlamps full on, Eve made her way towards the place she now knew, with its naked bulbs and three ancient petrol pumps. This time she did not stop, knowing that Dantang Plantation Hospital was only another half mile along the road. There, she pulled up and switched off the engine under the palm trees by the monsoon drain. She sat for a moment, listening to the crickets and to the night birds' melancholy call, and the beasts of the jungle.

Lisa was asleep. Anya and Zaina would have gone home hours ago. The horny claws of the lizards scuttered on the ceiling as Eve went into her hushed room above the hospital. She pulled off the sarong and laid it on a chair. It must have been years since she slept so sweetly and so deeply, naked under the thin coverlet. The sounds of the jungle were nothing so much as a lullaby, to tell her she was back home.

Eve woke next morning with a great hope and pleasure. Her first twenty-four hours had gone well at Dantang. Her own clothes were certainly not there, but Anya had laundered the blue sarong, and she dressed in it, and the gold Indian sandals that Mina Dalasingam had given her.

Eve was surprised to find the front room empty. Breakfast was laid and there was a pot of freshly-made green tea, a Chinese pot of traditional design, in turquoise china with wicker handles. The morning was beautiful, the buzzing of insects loud on the veranda, through the thin curtain where the sun streamed in through its delicate folds. Where was everyone? Eve ate some fruit thoughtfully and drank the tea. Outside, the monkeys chattered and the sun beamed down more harshly as morning progressed.

Had she offended Lisa Kai in some way? Where could the Malay girl be? Eve walked into the ward. Suky lay there, the remains of breakfast beside her.

'Hello, Suky. How do you feel?' Eve felt her fore-head. It seemed normal.

'I am well. Can I go home?'

'Yes, as soon as Sister Kai says so, my dear.'

The girl's almond eyes were appealing. 'Will she come soon?'

'Yes, very soon.'

But where was she? The hospital ought not to be left unattended. Eve stopped and glanced at Jacko. His face was as though carved from mahogany and she looked at him with compassion. She ought to stay with her patients. But something was wrong, Eve sensed it, and she had to go and look for the others. It must be important.

She looked outside. There was no one waiting under the trees, where yesterday there had been a queue of patients. Puzzled, Eve sat on the veranda, watching a courtship dance of two magnificent blue butterflies, darting and gliding among the shadows and sunlight. She looked at her watch. Almost eleven. Surely Zaina must be ill, not to have turned up for work? And how could Lisa leave her patients alone in the ward?

It might have been peaceful, sitting there in the sun, but as time wore on, Eve became more and more worried. If Lisa and Zaina were not here, they could only be in the village. If they were in the village, it could only be because there was some sort of emergency. She ought to go and see. It was wrong to sit here in the morning sun when there might be work to be done.

Having taken the decision, Eve took the precaution of

putting on sensible sandals and carrying her shoulder-bag, with a small first-aid kit inside it. Then she set off on foot, walking down the road to the village, knowing that it was only a few minutes away.

Dantang village could be heard before it could be seen. Those noisy chickens were still in good voice, she noticed. The dogs were silent. An indication, if one were needed, of the hottest time of the day. There were no cheerful children's voices either. A flock of doves took sudden fright at Eve's closeness and rose with a flurry above the trees as she approached.

Soon she was on the path that led to the middle of the village. It was strange that there was no one about, she thought. Perhaps it was too hot for the locals. But usually she would have expected to see a couple of children exchanging secrets in the shade, housewives talking, farmers returning for an afternoon sleep . . .

Then Eve heard a single voice, high and piercing in the distance, through the gentle clucking of the chickens. It was a man's voice, and it was shouting crazily, almost screaming. She quickened her step. If there was trouble, she might be needed. Then she came out of the shelter of the trees and found herself on the fringe of a group of silent villagers, all staring at the one figure in their midst. His black eyes were edged with white paint and he was holding forth in a stream of rapid Malay. He wore a quivering headdress of feathers on his ragged head, and round his naked chest was a thong on which were threaded three monkey skulls. He waved a long staff, which was painted black and white, and a monkey skull dangled from that also. Eve shivered. This must be the Bomoh.

Eve's Malay was painstakingly learned, and she found it hard to make out what was going on. Slowly she picked out Lisa Kai in the crowd, with Zaina and Anya close beside her. A woman beside Eve turned to look at her, and gasped openly. A few others turned to see what had caused her surprise. Soon more of the crowd had turned, and Eve heard the medicine man say her own name clearly—'Sister Carrol'. They were talking about her.

There was a young Malay with Lisa, a man Eve had not seen before. He wore western dress and his hair was stylishly cut, in the manner of the trendy young males of the towns. Lisa spotted Eve at that moment, and she grimaced and gestured to her not to come any closer.

And then the young man was at her side. 'Don't argue. I am a friend. Follow me, and try not to look back.' His urgent whisper communicated sudden fear to Eve. Whatever was going on in the village, it was not in her favour. She had no choice but to believe the young man.

'Is that the Bomoh?' she whispered.

'Too right. This way.' He slipped between two trees, into a rough part of the forest. Eve followed. It was bizarre and rather frightening. But she had seen him with Lisa, so he must be all right, and she had no choice but to put herself into his hands. She heard the voice of the Bomoh behind her, shouting madly, a high, hysterical chant. The man in front increased his pace and Eve ran after him, tripping on tree trunks and trailing plants, and setting small birds scurrying skywards in sudden startlement.

He stopped suddenly and leaned against a smooth palm trunk, panting. They seemed to be right in the middle of the jungle. Trees towered on all sides, leaving only a faint light filtering down through layers and layers of fronded foliage. 'You are Eve Carrol? I have not kidnapped the wrong lady?' He was out of breath, but he was reassuringly open faced and normal. 'Don't look so scared! I'm only the local chemist.'

'Chemist?' Eve wondered if she had heard properly.

'Sure. I own the pharmacy in Kuanang. I supply you. Didn't Lisa tell you about me?'

CHAPTER FOUR

THE man in front of her was Malay, his face smooth and square, defying any attempt to guess his age. He wore a short-sleeved white shirt and blue jeans, and his hair waved neatly into his slim neck. He was good-looking, with clear, honest eyes, and generous lips. He was watching Eve with a half-smile. 'Lisa Kai said I had to get you away from there. I hope I did the right thing.'

Eve nodded gratefully. 'Oh, yes, thank you. I almost expected to be carried off like Tarzan on one of those creeper things, and you to stand up and beat your chest.'

He acknowledged the joke with an intelligent grin. 'Miss Carrol, you don't know anything about the Bomoh, do you?'

'Nothing. I never heard the word until yesterday.'

'And yesterday you heard that there is a Bomoh in Dantang—and that he is a jealous so-and-so?'

She nodded again. 'Dr Craig said there was no love lost.'

'That is true. Myself, I find that modern medicine has learned to live with most Bomohs. Some are wise, and there are some things that only they can heal, among the villagers.' His face was serious now.

Eve responded. 'Of course. I am sure too. Any psychological illness might be helped by witch doctors.'

'Yes. Around here, there is what I call mutual toleration. Both kinds of doctors work together for the good of the people. That's as it should be. Unfortunately, our Bomoh here is a bit of an odd-ball, if you'll pardon my French.'

52

'But why is he so against me, for goodness' sake? What have I done? I've only just come here.' Eve sat down on a particularly comfortable-looking patch of soft moss on a fallen tree trunk. Somehow this man was easy to talk to. 'I only did one morning clinic. That's all.' She looked down at her feet in their sensible sandals, glad she had worn them. 'By the way, did you tell me your name?'

'I'm Balik. Pleased to meet you.' He held out his hand, and the handshake was firm and reliable. 'It isn't often I have the luck to meet such a pretty girl all to myself. Lisa always has that doctor fellow around.' He was joking, she knew, but there was some truth in his remarks.

'Well, I'm grateful for your help, Balik. Are you going to tell me why that crazy witch doctor of yours has taken a dislike to me?'

He had stripped a twig from a nearby tree and was carefully taking the bark from it, leaving a thin white taper of wood. He looked up under his shapely eyebrows. 'Jealousy, Eve, jealousy.'

'I honestly don't understand.'

He smiled down at her. 'It's stupid. But then, our Bomoh isn't very bright. Can you imagine what he felt when Mat Abdullah's mother came into the village singing your praises all over the place?'

Eve looked grim. 'I see. Even though I was only doing my job?'

He shook his head. 'He doesn't see it that way. He is saying, *lah*, that the reason you were able to save Mat's life is because you had cast the spell on him in the first place.'

Eve was silent for a while. Balik waited, understanding her feelings. Eve tried to smile as she shrugged her shoulders. 'Well, Balik, what do I do now?'

'Try not to worry. The villagers aren't stupid. They
have to listen to him when he dresses up and makes all
that fuss, but he can't do that all the time. You'll see.
They'll be back, as soon as their babies need injections,
or their cuts need stitching. Oh yes, they listen when the
Bomoh rants and raves—but he can't keep it up.'

'You mean this has happened before?'

'Not quite the same. But he did try to stop them
bringing their kids to the clinic. What happens? They
always come back. They know when they are getting
good treatment. The Bomoh hasn't twigged that yet.'

Eve sighed. 'Well, I hope this blows over.'

He pushed himself upright. 'So do I. Let me take you
home.'

'You've been very kind.' Eve stood up too. 'I'll be
glad to be back. To think I thought it might be routine,
working here.'

He smiled again, the white, even smile in the dark
olive face. 'Don't mention it. Just try not to save any
more lives in the next week or so. No dramatic dashes to
Jahin, and we'll get by.' They were both laughing now,
with the release of the tension, as Balik led the way
unerringly through the jungle paths towards the road to
the hospital.

They came to a wire fence. Balik vaulted over and
held out a hand to help Eve—who had never crossed a
fence in a sarong before. 'We are in the plantation now.
See? There are the trees that are being tapped. The ones
with V-shaped gashes in the trunks. Those little cups at
the bottom collect the latex as it oozes out.'

The trees were tall, with grey trunks bare of branches
up to six or seven feet above them. Eve watched,
fascinated, at the sap dripping from the gashed trunks,
dribbling into the wooden cups tied underneath.

There was a shout in the distance and Eve, still jumpy,

looked wary and backed away from the path. Balik said, 'No, no, it is all right. Only the plantation workers.'

They stood as a group of four women in brightly coloured sarongs came along the path, collecting the full cups and replacing them with empty ones. The women looked at them with little curiosity. After they had passed, Balik said, 'You see? These women don't give a hang what the Bomoh says. They listen when he is there but forget as soon as they leave him. They'll be at the clinic when they want you, you'll see.'

'Are you sure?'

'Trust me. By this time tomorrow it will all be over.'

They came out suddenly on to the main track. Eve said, delighted, 'I know where we are now. There's no need to trouble to come all the way.'

Balik looked disappointed. 'But I want to. And I need a cold drink.'

Eve laughed. 'Sorry. Forgive me. I was thoughtless.' They went on, and she said, 'You have someone looking after your shop in Kuanang?'

Balik shook his head cheerfully. 'No. I just don't open it. Customers will come again, if they really want something.'

Eve turned to look at the tranquil face, the smooth brow. 'I think you have told me in that sentence all I need to know about the East.'

'If you mean that we Malays don't believe in giving ourselves heart failure, then you are right. Life is a precious gift, Eve. It is for treasuring and enjoying, for living and loving, not for slaving and dying.' And four bright jays darted and sang, as though confirming the words of the young oriental philosopher. Eve smiled, and led the way to the veranda.

They were sitting, relaxed, drinking iced lemonade, when Lisa Kai appeared on the path and crossed the

monsoon drain to join them. Eve got up to meet her.
'Thank you for getting me out of that.'

To her surprise, Lisa did not seem pleased. She said
abruptly, 'Is there a bed ready? There is a child coming
in. I think she has glandular fever.'

Balik set his empty glass down. 'I'll be off, then. Any
more orders for me, lovely Lisa?'

She shook her head, not looking at him. 'I'll ring you.'

'*Baiklah. Selemat petang.*'

'Bye, Balik.' Her voice was cool. Balik lifted a hand to
each of the girls before running lightly down the steps,
across the bridge and down the road. Eve watched him
for a moment, admiring the litheness of his movements.
At Lisa's sullen silence, she turned back to the matter in
hand.

'Glandular fever, Lisa? Where do we get the blood
tests done?'

The other girl shook her head. 'This isn't the city.'

'I noticed,' said Eve drily, thinking of the mad Bomoh
and his necklace of skulls.

Lisa said sharply, 'Blood tests cost money. We will
know the diagnosis in a day or so, just by the symptoms.'

Eve pressed her lips together. This was not how she
had been trained. 'If you say so.'

They both went into the ward together, a distinct air of
coolness between them. Little Suky and old Jacko were
both sleeping. Lisa said shortly, 'This business with the
Bomoh—it could be serious, Eve. The Bomoh is so
powerful around here. People really do believe in magic,
you know.'

'But what can he say that makes sense?' Eve saw that
Lisa was taking it more to heart than Balik had.

Lisa said quietly, as she helped Eve fold a clean
bottom sheet on a bed, 'He is saying you caused the boy
to be ill. He says it is not reasonable for a boy who

looked so well to have any serious internal trouble. They believe him. He says that only a witch could have known.'

'He is calling me a witch?' Eve looked apprehensive as they drew the top cover over the white bed. 'Could you not explain referred pain to them? Surely it isn't all that difficult to understand?'

'It might have been easy—if the Bomoh hadn't got to them first. When I arrived, he was already accusing you. No one would listen to me.' She patted the pillow with more force than was needed and turned away to the partitioned alcove to fill in a record card for the patient she was expecting. Eve watched her with a feeling of foreboding. Lisa was going on, almost to herself, 'This Bomoh. I knew he would start something one of these days.'

Eve was very quiet after that. She felt that Lisa was almost accusing her of starting the trouble. She felt that she had lost a friend. When the mother arrived with the little girl with the glandular fever Lisa pointedly refused her help.

The child's name was Leila. She was attractive, shy, with wispy dark hair round a thin, honey-coloured face. Her throat was hurting and the glands in her neck were hard and painful. She insisted, on questioning, that she felt well. Eve saw that she was afraid of her mother. No wonder. The rubber workers were paid by the day, and a day off meant a loss of some ten or fifteen dollars.

It was late afternoon. They had settled the child in bed and given her and Suky some supper. There was suddenly a crackle of shots far in the jungle, a quick burst, like the one Eve had heard on her first night. It was followed by a huge flight of birds high above the trees. 'Lisa, what was that?'

But even such a dramatic sound did not change Lisa's

stony expression. She took away the children's dishes as though Eve had not spoken. She was deliberately not speaking, and Eve was puzzled and quite distressed. What had changed Lisa from the gracious and welcoming lady of the first night?

'Lisa, I think we should talk.'

'Not now. I'm busy.' And Lisa found minor tasks to do around the ward, which meant she did not have to make conversation. Eve watched her as though watching a total stranger. Surely the Bomoh's foolish accusations had not influenced Lisa, a sophisticated and intelligent woman? Perhaps she was jealous of the praise that Mat Abdullah's mother had heaped on Eve? The beautiful face was hostile, the manner coldly businesslike.

Eve tried to make conversation at dinner. 'Let's hope there is a nice long queue tomorrow morning. It hasn't been right, having no patients.'

'Yes.'

That had not worked. Eve tried again. 'When are you thinking of taking your leave?'

'Soon, I hope. My sister has written from Johore. She has a new baby, my second nephew, and she wants me to see how he has grown.' Lisa tried to answer normally, but her tone was subdued.

'Well, please don't worry about me. I am sure Zaina and Anya will give me all the help I need, if you want to go.'

But even that brought no response from Lisa. The meal became a silent affair, and the good food might have been sawdust for all Eve noticed what she ate.

Anya cleared the table. Lisa peeled a mango neatly and ate it slice by slice. Eve watched her, waiting for some indication of what was wrong. She again referred to Lisa taking her break. 'I know that I can always get hold of Dr Craig. I have memorised nearly all the telephone numbers written up by the phone.' No answer. 'And I have Balik's number, so that I can get in touch with him if we need anything in the pharmacy.'

'That won't be necessary.' Lisa's interjection was just a fraction too fast. 'The drug stocks are quite adequate. There would be no need to bother him. He is very busy in his shop. You should wait until I return.'

Eve felt greatly relieved as she looked again at the refined features of her companion, the glossy black hair tied in a pony tail down her straight back. Yes, there was definitely a hint of a blush as she spoke. Lisa Kai was jealous! Of course. She had come back and found Eve and Balik sitting together on the veranda, drinking lemonade together, laughing and chatting like old friends. Lisa had been jealous, because she was fond of Balik herself. To make it more sure, Eve deliberately repeated his name. 'Nice chap, Balik. Good-looking.'

'You like him?' Lisa's voice was hard.

'Not specially. But he was kind. Do you like him?'

'Well, he is very popular.' Again, Eve sensed more in the simple remark than Lisa said. Yes, Balik was popular—he was so easy to talk to, so jolly and out-going. He must visit many clinics and surgeries, chat up many nurses and receptionists. Lisa liked him a lot, that was clear now. And most probably, thought she had very little chance of landing this handsome butterfly. Eve's presence had only made it even more difficult.

She knew she had to clear the air. Standing up casually, she said, 'Popular or not, he is certainly not my type.' And she walked out through the muslin curtain and sat in the shadows on the veranda, watching the moonlight silvering the tops of the trees, and reflecting off the metal bridge. After a few moments Lisa came out and sat quietly in the next chair. Peace had been declared, to Eve's great relief.

'You know, Lisa, I object to being called a witch.'

The other woman was more relaxed now. She said calmly, 'There is no need to worry too much. These people soon forget. When they need us, they will come. You will soon learn the ways of these country folk—they are different from the city. They have no pretence. They are simple and uncomplicated by any desire other than self-preservation.'

Eve said thoughtfully, 'I wonder if Dr Craig understands the people the way you do?'

Lisa shook her head. 'Maybe. Maybe not. Don't you see? He doesn't have to. He cures the diseases of the body. It is we—we who have to nurse the real people behind the diseases, who must be able to understand them.'

Eve smiled. 'You are quite fond of Dr Craig, aren't you?' She watched the delicate face in the moonlight. No blush, or embarrassment at that comment. No, Dr Craig was not prominent in Lisa's thoughts.

The Malay girl pulled down a trailing creeper and rolled and unrolled one of the scented leaves as she spoke. 'Fond is not the right word. He is a remote man. I admire him very much. He is a good doctor and he is full of integrity. He would never do anything against his conscience.'

Eve wondered if this were true. There was a lot about Andrew Craig that she could not explain. She thought of the man he had met out here in the darkness; the man in combat gear who had summoned him with a low whistle—the same as had happened at Abbas's garage. She recalled how Dr Craig had passed her on the road— and yet had turned up at the garage after she had already arrived . . . Where had he been, and why had she not seen him on that lonely road? 'He gives the impression of being remote. But sometimes people like that have a guilty secret, Lisa,' she said idly.

Lisa sat impassive, a picture now of oriental serenity. 'You must look at the man closely, Eve. You must believe he is good. Otherwise you will never be happy at Dantang.'

Eve grinned in the darkness. 'I promise I will. And when you go on leave, I will make sure I run things so well that he decides there is no need for him to come back.'

Lisa managed a smile. 'That is for him to say.'

'Agreed. I might just help him make his mind up. He is one gentleman I find completely dispensable in my life.'

It was with good humour that the two girls went indoors. So much for their minor disagreement. Eve was relieved that they did not have to quarrel over Balik. She liked Lisa and would not want to lose her friendship. Eve lay on her bed that night, watching the blades of the fan swish by. It had been a disturbing first two days. But her main feeling was one of peace. She was glad she had saved one young life and that her relationships here were proving manageable. Dantang, though not paradise, was still a place that tugged at her inner longings and needs.

Next morning, Zaina turned up as though nothing had happened. They sent her to the village to take Suky home. 'You see?' Lisa had said, 'The villagers have short memories. You will see. There will be people under the banana tree before morning is much hotter.'

Little Leila was no better. Lisa said, 'There can be little doubt that it's glandular fever. I ought to inform Dr Craig.'

'A Paul Bunel test would tell you definitely.'

'And what good will that do? There is no treatment, anyway. We must just keep her comfortable and hope that with good nursing she improves quickly.' Leila's mother had come from the village, forgetting about losing wages. She brought her fruit and candies and sat beside her, wiping her forehead and smoothing the pillows.

'You don't mind her here?' Eve whispered. 'Suppose she gives the child something wrong?'

'That is where eastern and western medicine differ,' replied Lisa. 'Maybe in the West mothers do not mind strangers looking after their children. Here in Dantang, we think the best person to care for a child is her own mother.'

Eve admitted she might be right. There could be no harm, so long as trained nurses were close by. Slowly, but surely, she was absorbing the philosophy of Dantang and losing the strict rules she had been trained to follow.

'I think I will go down to the garage and see if there is any sign of my lost suitcase.'

'Very well.' But as the two women came out into the sunshine, there, in the clearing, were three patients waiting quietly under the trees. Lisa said, her voice relieved and light, 'What did I tell you? The Bomoh doesn't frighten anyone here for very long. Let's go and get the desks out.'

Eve felt her heart lighten. The people didn't think any harm of her. She could still do the job she came here to do. She looked at the square, village faces with pleasure, listened to their subdued chatter, the trilling of the jays in the trees and the far gabble of monkeys. This was what she had come for. She was smiling to herself as she smoothed down her sarong and took her seat under the shade of the veranda for her first patient.

Lisa came out. 'Would you like to do this one single-handed?'

Eve nodded. 'Oh, yes. The sooner the better.'

'Then I will go to the village for you. I want some other things. Zaina is looking after the ward, so you should have a straightforward morning.'

'Thank you.' This was her first chance to show she could do the job. Eve went back to taking her patient's blood pressure. As she listened to the pulsing blood in the arm with the stethoscope, she saw Lisa walking down into the shadow of the jungle road, the figure trim and graceful, the hair swept up, glossy and exotic. Balik would be a fool, she thought, if he didn't realise what a woman Lisa was.

There was a shout and then a babble of voices in the direction of the plantation. Eve took no notice at first. There was often laughing and shouting as the workers enjoyed themselves. But then a young boy came running like a hare towards the hospital. Behind him there appeared a group of women in their vividly coloured sarongs. The boy reached her, panting. 'Come, hurry. One lady hurt bad, bleed a lot, *lah*!'

Eve saw then that the women were surrounding another who was holding her arm. As they came closer she realised that the red blotches on the yellow sarong were not a pattern, but great patches of blood which was spurting from a cut, staining her hand and arm bright scarlet. 'Zaina, I need you out here!' Eve grabbed a cotton tourniquet and ran to meet the women. She wrapped it round the upper arm, pressing on the cut artery with all her strength. Zaina came scurrying out to help. She bound a length of bandage round the wound, while Eve continued to stem the bleeding at the artery. As they held the woman, they led her gently across the bridge and laid her on the grass.

'Want her in the ward?' asked Zaina.

'No. Stop the bleeding first.' The woman had been

moaning a little, mainly from fear, but now she fell
silent. Eve wasn't sure if it was through weakness or
because she felt she was now with someone who could
help her. She said to one of the woman, 'How long has
she been bleeding like this?'

'Just now. We bring her, number one quick.'

'I hope so.' They must have walked a quarter of a mile
from the plantation. Eve watched the redness staining
the bandage that Zaina held. Suddenly the telephone
rang. 'Oh, take no notice.' She couldn't spare anyone at
that moment. After it had rung and rung, Eve turned
to one of the village women, still trying to exert pressure on the bleeding arm. 'Please answer the telephone. Say I am very busy and take the number. I'll
ring back.'

The woman went in to get the phone, which was close
to the front door. 'Hello? Yes?' Eve only half listened.
She felt her muscles aching with the force she was
applying to the artery with the tourniquet. Was that
ominous red stain at last ceasing to grow larger? Had
they halted the urgent pulsing of blood? If not, then they
had an emergency on their hands. The woman would
need transfusing. Eve lifted her face briefly. There was
no sign of Lisa returning from the village.

The woman moaned again. Eve looked down, sweat
running into her eyes. 'Don't worry. We will get you into
the ward now.' She slowly removed the bandage. Yes,
the bleeding had been stemmed. Eve did not loose the
tourniquet as she looked carefully at the still seeping cut.
'I think it would be just as well if I put in a couple of
stitches before moving you.'

The patient spoke, through dry lips. 'You are nurse
who look after Mat Abdullah?'

Eve's heart sank. She had been listening to the
Bomoh. She was not going to allow Eve to treat her. She

said slowly, 'Yes, I took him to the hospital. It was Mr Dalasingam who cured him by operating.'

She watched the reaction from the square, attractive face of her patient. The Bomoh must have said some very powerful things against Eve. But the woman's worried frown began to smooth out. The corners of the dry mouth turned up and her face cleared. She beamed with a sudden confidence and trust, and Eve felt an overwhelming sense of release. 'I thought—' Then she stopped. There was no point is mentioning her fears. The woman's smile said it all. Lisa had been right. The Bomoh made a big noise in the village, but the people knew what was really good for them.

Eve called Zaina to take charge of the tourniquet. 'Now, you must keep still. I must get the edges of the skin cleanly together.' With brisk movements, she reached for an emergency suturing kit and took out the antiseptic to clean the wound. Although it stung, and she saw the patient flinch, the woman said nothing, but bravely lay perfectly still and allowed Eve to clean the wound properly, apply liberal iodine and draw the edges together with four firm stitches. She covered it finally with an antiseptic dressing.

Sweat poured down Eve's face as she worked. Midday was upon them, and though the veranda gave shade, the heat was oppressive. She used her forearm to wipe the sweat and worked patiently until she was sure the bleeding had been contained. Then she gave permission for the woman to be moved to the ward, to have her blood-soaked clothes removed gently and a hospital gown slipped on.

Eve straightened up, feeling the aching in her back ease off as her body recovered from the enormous tension she had applied for so long. Anya brought her a glass of water from the fridge. 'I make coffee?' But Eve shook her head and went into the ward.

The woman smiled from her neat white bed, her arm swathed in clean white bandages. Two of her friends sat by the bed, but went away obediently when Eve explained that she must rest now. 'She can be taken home tomorrow, if all is well.'

Soon the ward was silent but for the woman's deep breathing. Eve felt her own eyes begin to grow heavy. She went over to the still form of Jacko. When she saw his eyes open, she bent to speak to him. 'Water? Would you like some soup?'

He tried to speak, but was out of practice. She bent and assisted him to take some water. He fell back on the pillows, too weak to do anything. Eve shook her head. He ought to be on intravenous fluids. It was wrong for him to be left there like a load of old washing, with no one taking any notice of him. Ill or not, it was against her instincts to leave anyone to die.

She brought the sphygmomanometer from the office and wrapped the cuff round the thin arm. 'Oh dear, Jacko, this blood pressure is very low.' He had fallen back on the pillow, still as a corpse. She put her stethoscope back in her ears and listened to his chest. His heart was still going. But there were disturbing signs of a chest infection.

Footsteps sounded on the metal bridge outside. Eve was just removing the stethoscope when Dr Craig strode in and walked right over to her. The blue eyes were dark with disapproval. 'I telephoned an hour ago. It's rather fortunate there was nothing urgent I wanted to say, isn't it, Sister Carrol?'

Eve glared at him, furious. How dare he talk to her like that! She opened her mouth, but did not trust herself to speak. Her heart thumping violently, she stood up and swept past him without a word. She did not wish to speak to Andrew Craig now, and never would. There could be nothing she would ever have in common with him.

CHAPTER FIVE

THE atmosphere between Eve and her chief was electric with dislike. And the trouble was that they would have to eat tonight at the same table. As Eve showered and changed into her other borrowed sarong, she tried to calm the irregular beating of her heart. She had dealt with bad-tempered doctors before, so she ought not to find him quite so disturbing. Perhaps it was because they were so isolated here—so dependent upon each other for company and conversation. She could only hope that Lisa was feeling chatty tonight.

Dr Craig had taken some papers from his car and gone up to his room. Eve relaxed slightly and joined Lisa on the veranda as the sun dived steeply in a glow of scarlet behind the trees, setting the jungle on fire for a few glorious moments. 'What a place,' Eve murmured. 'But how do you stand it when he is around?'

'Dr Craig?' Lisa smiled slightly. 'Would you believe me if I said that he isn't usually like that. Not to me, anyway.' She looked down modestly as she spoke, and again Eve wondered how close the relationship could be between Craig and Lisa. She was such a pretty woman. And Craig had said he preferred oriental women, hadn't he?

Anya was setting the table in the front room. They heard her humming to herself as she placed the cutlery out and smoothed the pure white cloth. The crickets were beginning their nightly serenade as the last streaks of daylight faded into a velvet night. 'What is he doing up in his room, Lisa?' Eve asked.

Lisa stood up and walked to the veranda rail. She looked lovely in a dark blue sarong edged with a yellow and black border. She stood like some oriental princess, calm and still, her glossy hair piled up, showing off the slim neck and throat. Eve thought that even stony old Craig could not help but notice her beauty.

'I suppose he is writing up his notes. He's doing some research on anaemia in the villages for the *Journal of Tropical Medicine*.' She turned round and sat on the rail, holding on to the wooden pillars of the veranda, where the orchids and creepers wound round. 'Tell me about yourself, Eve. What made you come so far out into the wilds?'

A dark voice spoke from the doorway, and Andrew Craig moved out elegantly to join them. 'I find English women who come out here are either running away from something, or are a bunch of idealistic do-gooders. I wonder which category you fit into, Sister Carrol?' As he sat down in the bamboo chair vacated by Lisa, Anya came out with a tray, on which were three glasses and a small glass jug. Craig waited until it was placed on the table and then poured an amber liquid from the jug. He handed a glass to Lisa first, and then looked up at Eve. 'You'll join us? It is a prescription of my own, which we have found suits us best in this climate.'

Eve nodded, noticing that he said 'we', indicating a longstanding friendship with Lisa. She sipped the drink, finding it a version of sweet Martini, but more tangy and refreshing. She noticed that Craig had not waited for a reply to his rudely phrased question. It was perhaps just as well, for she herself was not sure of the answer. Was she running away? It had not occurred to her before. Had the affair with Michael hurt her more than she realised? Was it Michael she was running from, and not the luxury life in KL that bored her? She was glad of the glass to hold, to look down on, so that she could hide the sudden flush of uncertainty in her cheeks.

In the silence, she found herself saying, 'I'd be interested to know about your research, Doctor.'

He looked across, apparently surprised. 'You would? It is pretty simple. I thought it would be useful to correlate into tables the incidence and causes of some blood abnormalities out here. Of course, in places like India there is a lot of bacterial activity. But here the villages are provided with good water supplies, and the causes are mainly nutritional.'

Anya called them to the table. As they stood up, Eve suddenly stiffened. A man's figure slipped out of the shelter of the trees, and then swiftly back again. She was sure it was the same man she had seen speaking to Craig. She looked at him. He did not appear to have noticed anything.

'What is it?' he asked, irritably.

'It's nothing. I thought I saw something . . .' Eve turned and followed Lisa indoors, brushing past the thin muslin curtain that kept out the insects. She was sure it was a man. And yes—there had been a low whistle just before he appeared. She had only been conscious of the jungle noises, but the whistle was like that of a bird.

Andrew Craig helped himself to the grilled satay on bamboo sticks, and dipped it in the dish of hot sauce. He did not comment at all on Eve's remark. Turning to Lisa, he said, 'You're due for some leave, aren't you?'

'Yes. When Eve knows the routine, I'll take it.'

'She should be all right. I'll be here. I shall be staying for several days yet.' He looked across the table at Eve, his blue eyes telling her nothing. She was very conscious of his handsome presence, conscious that she had never felt such a response to any man before. Good looks were not a priority with Eve. She rated kindness and courtesy, a sense of humour, more than mere outward appearances. She felt her heart jump as he said he was staying on. Was it annoyance or perhaps relief that she would not be left alone? She certainly felt more nervous, now that she had seen the strange, mysterious figures in the jungle. Even Craig's dour company was better than none.

Eve said firmly, 'Yes, Lisa. You make your arrangements. I'll be fine. I'll soon pick up the routine.'

Andrew Craig helped himself to rice before belatedly offering the dish to Eve. 'I hope you will soon pick up a decent uniform also.'

She answered shortly, 'I don't think my nursing will improve.'

To her surprise, he spoke more gently. 'No. But I think the patients have more faith in your qualifications. That is, until they get to know you better.' And it seemed a reasonable comment. Why hadn't he spoken more politely the first time?

Anya brought in a tray with cups and saucers. 'Missy Carrol like coffee or tea?'

'I don't mind at all.'

Lisa laughed. 'That will be music in Anya's ears. The doctor is adamant that coffee is the only drink for after dinner. And I insist on having my green tea. So you see, Anya leaves us to make our own.'

Craig was actually smiling then, looking across to Lisa, his face transformed by the open, relaxed expression. 'But that is the only thing we disagree about, isn't it?'

And Eve was quick to notice the warmth and genuine affection in Lisa's almond eyes as she smiled back. Lisa might not admit it, but Andrew Craig was more than a mere colleague to her. For a moment Eve felt like an outsider, intruding on these two who looked into each other's eyes for a brief but telling couple of seconds. Then Lisa said, 'I'll just see to the patients before I have my tea.'

Eve stood up. 'I'll come.'

'No, Eve, not tonight. You must be tired. Anya will come with me. She sleeps next to the ward, and is our permanent night sister.'

'I *am* tired,' Eve admitted, and as Lisa left the room, Craig stood up. He moved out to the veranda. Eve said, 'Good night, sir.'

He looked back. 'You won't join me for coffee, then?'

She wanted to. But she had been unsettled enough for one night. He might ask her more searching questions about herself. And Eve knew she was not ready to answer any. Especially as he was regarding her now with a more frank expression, looking her up and down, making her acutely conscious of the clinging sarong over her slim hips, the low neck that was more revealing than Eve usually wore. She murmured a reply. Craig gave a curt nod and turned on his heel and she was left staring at a gently swinging curtain.

Eve went upstairs on silent bare feet. She prepared for bed and lay on top of the cover, for in spite of the fan, it was stiflingly hot. She listened to the clatter as Anya cleared the table and could hear the low sound of voices, as Lisa and Andrew Craig chatted together over their cups. They seemed to stay out there a long time, and there was a feeling of intimacy about their murmuring voices and their occasional gentle laughter. She heard Lisa come upstairs at last, whispering past her door. Then everything went very quiet, but for the cicada chorus around the lonely hospital.

She was awakened later. She didn't know why. The moon was high, silvering the walls of her little room, and the wind was getting up, making the treetops rustle all around them. Suddenly she heard a metallic click. Eve crept out of bed and looked out at the silver jungle, bathed in moonlight. There, by the Rover, stood Dr Craig. He had opened the boot of the car and took out a couple of medicine bottles before closing the boot as quietly as he could. The moon slipped behind a ragged cloud, but not before she had seen him walking purposefully towards the jungle.

The doctor was not at breakfast next morning. Lisa was visibly happy to be taking her leave. 'Could you manage on your own this morning, Eve? I'd like to go down to the village, to buy some local wood-carvings for my sophisticated sister. And something for the baby, of course.'

'I'd love to manage on my own. Stay as long as you like.' Eve thought to herself that if Andrew Craig stayed away too, it would be even better. 'When you pass Abbas's, would you ask him if there is any sign of my missing suitcase?'

'Sure. Anything else?'

Eve grinned ruefully. 'Maybe you'd better get me a cotton dress or two. Attila the Hun seems to dislike me wearing your clothes.' She looked down at the freshly-laundered sarong that Anya had laid out for her.

'Oh, he doesn't mean it. You mustn't mind his gruff ways, Eve. He is really the kindest man in the world.' Lisa's dark eyes shone with affection. Eve felt a stab of envy. She wished she could share some of the Malay girl's obvious pleasure in having Andrew Craig as her boss.

'Well,' Eve said, ignoring Lisa's last remark, 'I'd better do a ward round. Two patients or twenty, they must be seen regularly.'

'If you like.' Lisa sounded offhand. 'But Zaina sees to them. I only go if I'm needed.'

Eve said softly, 'Is that your country ways? Would you mind if I introduced just one or two city ideas while I am here? I promise not to upset your general routine.'

Lisa looked across at her, and her face was impassive. 'I can't argue with you when I'm on holiday, so I suppose you will have to do what you think is right. But, Eve, be careful before you change things. We've worked here for three years without any trouble. It works, our system.'

'Your system. Yours and Craig's?'

Lisa corrected her swiftly. '*Doctor* Craig, you mean.'

'I'm sorry.' Eve didn't want to tread on any toes while she was still the new girl, even though she was critical of the easy-going routine. 'I'll just take a quick look at the ward, all the same. Just for my own satisfaction.'

'Sure.'

The subject was closed. Lisa went down to the village and Eve washed her hands and went along to the little ward. Zaina was sitting in the alcove, watching the three occupied beds. The child lay still, eyes brighter but her body listless, her little hands on the white coverlet, not interested in the book that lay open on the bed.

'*Salaam*. Good morning, Zaina. How are things?'

'Fine, Sister Carrol. The child's temperature is still raised. Mrs Pande is fine, and wants to go home.'

'And Jacko?'

Zaina looked blank. 'He is there.'

'What is his temperature?'

'I do not know.'

Eve could not help sighing. If this had been Kuala Lumpur she would have been furious because a routine test had not been carrried out. But here, in Dantang, she knew that old Jacko had been given up for lost. He was in the ward, but he didn't count. For a brief moment Eve was furious. Then her philosophical side took control.

'Okay, Zaina. I'll do it.'

Mrs Pande had lifted herself in her hospital bed as Eve approached. 'Sister, I am well. Let me go home.'

Eve went over to her. She knew very well that the woman was wanting to get back to work, hating the waste of time stuck in bed for nothing. She went to her at once. 'I'm glad to see you so lively. Let's have a look at this cut.' She began to unwind the bandages. It was encouraging, the fact that the outer bandages were not bloodstained. She revealed the wound. 'Hmm. Not bad, Mrs Pande. I do believe I can let you go. But please stay off work for another day at least. Just to make sure.' With deft fingers, Eve redressed the cut with a lighter bandage. 'Now, I must see you in a week. And come back at once if you feel ill, okay?'

'Oh, yes, Sister. Thank you, Sister, *terimasakih*.'

Eve looked up at Zaina, who stood at her side. 'I think it would be safer if you walked back with Mrs Pande.'

'Yes, Sister.' Zaina smiled at the patient, as a huge grin spread over her face. 'Come, I help you get dressed.' Eve could not help noticing that the yellow sarong, which last night had been covered with browny-red bloodstains, had been laundered by the motherly Anya and lay on the chair, neatly ironed. Eve was impressed. That would not happen in KL. The maids did nothing on their own initiative. Maybe she was learning more of the country way of nursing. And maybe it did have some good points, after all.

While all this had been going on, Eve found herself beginning to get worried. Why had Andrew Craig not come down? She thought he would have been delighted to be there on her first ward round, anxious to find fault with her because of her inappropriate dress. She went over to Leila and inspected her throat, took her pulse and her temperature again.

Anya appeared at the entrance to the ward. 'Sister, I will be going to the village for some provisions.'

Eve turned. 'Has Sister Kai gone?'

'Yes.' That was a pity. Otherwise, Lisa could have taken Mrs Pande. 'All right, Anya. Wait for Zaina. You can take Mrs Pande together.' It would mean that Eve was on her own for the morning clinic, but she didn't mind that. In any case, Dr Craig would probably be up by now, more than ready to follow Eve around and find fault with her work.

After they had gone, the ward was very quiet. Eve was alone in the hospital except for Andrew Craig. She looked at her watch. It was after eleven. She began to feel distinctly uneasy. Surely the doctor should have been down by now?

Hardly realising what she was doing, Eve went upstairs to the corridor and listened again. There was no sound at all. And in spite of her aversion to the dour Scot, Eve found herself apprehensive. Surely, if he were here, he would at least have gone along to the bathroom? She resolutely walked to his door and tapped on it.

There was a crash in the room, as though something had fallen over. But no human voice. Eve tried the door handle. It opened, and she put her head nervously inside. Then she gasped and rushed in. Andrew Craig lay there, dressed only in the light grey trousers he had worn last night. He was crumpled in a frightening way on his bed, and at the bedside was a phial, a syringe and a bottle of surgical spirit.

For one single second, she suspected the worst. A drug addict, who had overdone it. But then she was immediately ashamed of her thoughts, for one look at him confirmed that his lips and eyelids were swollen in a typical allergic reaction. He was poisoned. She felt his pulse. It was almost non-existent. With thumping heart, she swiftly took his blood pressure with his own sphig. 'Oh, God. No, don't let him die!' she murmured unconsciously to herself.

Something was badly wrong. Eve looked at the phial beside the bed. Hydrocortisone! He must have been going to inject himself. She picked up the syringe. One hundred milligrams. Yes, she knew that was the treatment for anaphylactic shock. And she knew, too, that untreated it could be fatal. Firmly she took control of her shaking hands. She picked up the syringe and checked that the contents were easily injected. Then she took the doctor's brown arm and searched for the easiest vein. It was not hard, for he was lean and his veins were throbbing weakly under the skin of the tanned arm, with its downy covering of dark hairs.

Feeling icy cool, she looked once more at the dark face with its closed, puffy eyelids, the apparent absence of breathing. There was nothing for it, the injection was his only hope. Slowly, she pierced the skin with the needle and found the congested vein. Agonisingly slowly, as the drug was coursed round his body, the swollen eyelids flickered and opened. Eve withdrew the empty syringe and reached for the swarthy wrist, praying desperately for a pulse.

It was there! Shaky at first, but with dramatic speed the pulse throbbed and returned to normal as the life-saving drug revived the pale body. Eve found herself holding both his hands in hers and squeezing them in relief. He was going to be all right.

There was a moan from his swollen lips. Hastily she reached for a tumbler of water from the bedside table. Holding his head gently, she administered the liquid very slowly. Setting the glass down, she turned and saw that the blue eyes were open and returning almost visibly to normal. 'Eve. You found . . . ?'

She nodded. 'The hydrocortisone was there. I thought—you must have got it for yourself, sir.'

His lips were still slightly swollen, but he said with a hint of humour, 'You call all your patients sir?'

She looked down into the lean face, the blue sapphires of his eyes. She shook her fair curls, smiling in relief at his recovery. 'No.'

His arm came out, caught her in a gentle grip, and held her against his body, so that she sensed the rhythm of his heartbeat and rejoiced in its return to a strong, steady rhythm. She lay there against him for what seemed like ages, as though neither of them wished to separate. This arrogant stranger had undergone a metamorphosis. In the desperate crisis they had both endured, it was as though they had welded together into a single, vital relationship.

Slowly, reluctantly, Eve raised her head and looked into his face, now restored to its original handsome features. 'You feel okay?'

In reply, he struggled, the muscles twisting in his superb body, and sat upright against the pillows. 'There.' And in response to her impulsive smile of delight, he took her hand in a now strong grip. 'Eve, if you hadn't come . . .' He left the rest unsaid, but she knew without being told. 'It was a sting. Some insect. It might even have been a snake, but I'm usually very careful about where I step . . .'

She did not take her hand away. Somehow it seemed awfully right for them to be clinging to each other at that moment. 'Now I see what Lisa meant when she said not to go into the jungle.'

Andrew Craig looked at her, and there was no hardness in his eyes. She knew that he realised she had seen him last night. He made no attempt to explain. 'Would you ask Anya to bring me some tea?'

'She isn't here. I'm alone. I'll get it.'

'Alone?'

Eve explained where everyone was. 'There must be quite a queue for me under the banana trees by now.' She left him. She did not look back, but she ran downstairs with a light step, feeling that now, at least, they had established a bond between them. There could surely be no more tension, no more resentment. She had saved him from some allergic reaction to an insect sting that might have proved fatal if she had not felt that something was wrong and gone up to him at that precise moment.

She took up a large mug of green tea. Andrew Craig was standing up, now dressed in a fresh cotton shirt. He had shaved, and the scent of his aftershave lingered in the room. Eve handed the tea to him.

'You are all right now?' she asked.

'I'm fine.' He took the mug from her, and with his other hand he took hers. 'You are trembling, Eve.' The devastating eyes looked deep into hers.

'Just reaction,' she mumbled, and tried to take her hand away. But he held on to it.

'I—I—have to go. The patients are waiting.'

'Here.' He made her sip from his mug before he would take some himself. 'You need it as much as I do.'

'I'm fine, Dr Craig, really.'

'Yes, Eve, you really are.' And as she looked up at the unusually gentle words, the tall doctor stooped and touched her still trembling lips with his own. 'Thanks, Eve. Thank you.'

She walked downstairs again. This time there was no sign of the usual calm. Eve's heart raced, and she touched her fingers to her mouth where he had kissed it. It burned with a feeling she had never experienced before, as though it was the very first time she had been kissed. And that was nonsense, because Michael had kissed her many times, and she had honestly thought she had enjoyed it. But now, as she walked towards her waiting patients, she knew that this one single touch had proved that she had been right to leave Michael, right to forget him, and right to come here, so many miles from civilisation.

It was after one by the time she had finished seeing to the villagers. Eve wrote up their records conscientiously. Then she took the morning's notes indoors, and began to file them in alphabetical order in the small alcove off the ward. She felt calm now, and very happy. There was a total sense of satisfaction that filled her with exhilaration. She could do the job she came for. And she could do it well, alone, without help and without any further trouble from the others. Surely now, Andrew Craig would treat her as he treated Lisa, with affectionate consideration. Eve felt her cheeks glow at the way he had treated her this morning.

There was a sudden noise of coughing from the ward. Eve turned, expecting it to be little Leila. It must be glandular fever, she felt certain by now. Poor child. But the outburst had come from Jacko, and now he lay, eyes closed, as though the cough were his final protest to the world.

Eve grabbed the stethoscope. His chest rattled and his breathing was diminished, especially in the lower lobes. Eve looked again at the lifeless face, the bones standing out in his cheeks, forehead and nose. Alarmed, she knew she could not let the poor, trusting fellow lie here and die. She ran to the phone, checking the list on the wall. There, clearly, was *Ambulan* and a Jahin number. She dialled decisively.

'I have a patient with pneumonia. Can you admit him

to the General Hospital?'

'Is it urgent?'

'Yes.'

'I will send a vehicle as soon as I can.'

'*Terimasakih*.' There. It had been easy. The ambulance was on its way. And as it was coming so far, Eve decided not to waste the journey. She went to Leila. 'My dear, I need to take a tiny drop of blood for the hospital in Jahin to help you. Will you be good for just a second?' And as the child watched her with eyes bright with temperature, Eve drew off a sample of blood and discharged it into a phial specially prepared. She wrote Leila's name on it, and the name of Dantang Hospital.

The ramshackle ambulance was there within the hour. Eve carefully supervised the transfer of old Jacko to a stretcher, and thence to the waiting vehicle. 'Thank you. And this—please get the lab to do a Paul Bunel test. I have written it on the paper.'

The ambulance disappeared round the bend in the road down to Dantang. Eve's heart felt light. She knew she had done the right thing. She turned to go back into the hospital as the heat of the midday sun penetrated the thatched veranda.

Andrew Craig was standing there, crisply dressed. His face was stern. 'That was Jacko?' Eve nodded, disturbed at his words, which dripped with ice. 'You didn't think of consulting me first?'

CHAPTER SIX

AND THAT was all he said about Jacko. For the rest of that day Andrew Craig addressed no word to Eve, though he chatted normally with Lisa when she returned, and with Zaina about the patients. Eve tried to be philosophical. Well, he didn't really like me anyway. He had to be nice to me because I happened to be there in time to give him an injection, she thought. All the same, she found it hurt a little to see the gentle way he spoke to Lisa about her forthcoming holiday, and about her family.

'Have you made your travel arrangements, Lisa? Your plane is booked?'

'Yes. I'll have to leave here tomorrow afternoon. The flight to Singapore is at six in the evening.' Eve felt her heart sink. Without Lisa, life here would be one long, silent battle of wills, she could see. She looked across the dinner table, where Andrew Craig was helping himself to one of Anya's beautifully cooked vegetable pancakes. He showed no interest in her at all, and she wondered if she had imagined the gentle clasp of his arms as he had held her close against his chest, her cheek against the hard tanned body.

He said, dissecting the pancake with delicate, fastidious fingers, 'And how are you getting to KL?'

A slight flush touched Lisa's peach-like complexion. 'I think Balik will be coming for me. He will telephone tonight.' She did not raise her eyes from her plate, and Eve admired the way the silky eyelashes curled naturally.

Andrew said calmly, 'Well, don't worry. I can take you.'

'Thank you.'

'You will be able to do the morning clinic?'

Lisa nodded. 'Oh yes. My packing is already done.'

'That would be helpful. I'd like to take Sister Carrol down to the village.'

'Me?' Eve started. She had not expected Andrew Craig to take any notice of her.

For the first time that evening he looked straight at her, and she felt the force of those direct blue eyes, intelligent and with the power to disturb her more than she cared for. 'You did say you were interested in my research?'

'Oh, yes.' She meant it. And she was on safer ground now. He was apparently not going to scold her any more about the Jacko affair. Her feelings lifted a notch. Perhaps it wasn't going to be too bad after all, working with Dr Craig, if he was going to treat her like a human being at last. 'You have some patients in the village?'

He nodded. 'I'll show you the notes later. One boy of twelve, who I think had simple iron-deficiency anaemia. I don't expect any further trouble from him, now I've explained the importance of a balanced diet to his mother.'

'But isn't iron-deficiency anaemia uncommon in males?'

The doctor almost smiled. 'You are right. That is why I have included him in my study. We'll follow him up for twelve months and make sure there is nothing else wrong.'

Eve said, rather wickedly, 'But how can you follow up these people without proper pathology lab facilities?'

He looked at her gravely. She knew he had taken the point. But he was too mature to rise to the bait.

'You don't need a lab to take a case history, Sister Carrol.'

'And is that what you want me to do?'

'Yes, please.'

Things were looking up. Not only had he talked to her with professional equality, he had also said 'please'. Encouraged, she asked, 'Any other patients in Dantang?'

'There is a chap with tropical sprue. He responded well to injections of vitamin B12, but I want him to stay on a gluten-free diet, and as he is not too bright, I doubt if he has managed it.'

'Is sprue common here?'

'No. And of course, the origin of the damage to the intestine isn't known. We must just keep a check on the known cases and be wary of other complications.'

'Doesn't infection from some tapeworms cause malabsorbtion?'

He seemed amused. 'You *have* done your homework, Sister Carrol! But mostly it is the fish tapeworm, and the people in the villages do not eat much fish. It is more common in coastal communities, and the west coast is more highly developed than the east, so the east is where the tapeworm can be a cause.' He finished his rice thoughtfully, and laid down his fork. 'You naturally studied these diseases before you came out here?'

Eve felt a rush of emotion as she remembered the enthusiasm of those months, when she knew she was coming out to join Michael in KL. She had read her tropical medicine thoroughly while she was getting her job fixed up, having her inoculations and arranging for her work permit. It had been such an exciting time . . . only to come to nothing when she had arrived and seen in Michael's face that he no longer felt as he used to. He had fallen out of love. She didn't blame him, but it hadn't been easy to carry on working with the same enthusiasm. Not at first.

Andrew Craig said quietly, 'You don't answer. Have I hit on a nerve?'

Eve faced him. 'You were right, Doctor. I believe I did come out here because I was running away from something.' There. She had admitted it. Now it would be easier to bear. But she didn't want any more questions about it now. Eve stood up and excused herself from the table. She went hurriedly outside, brushing past the delicate curtain and glad of the softness of the velvet night.

It was all wrong to be recalling all this, just as the pain had started to ease. She had thought all that would be left behind as soon as she left the comforts and luxuries of the capital behind her and took the jungle road to Dantang.

Eve sat looking out towards the jungle, but she saw nothing. Her reverie was deep and somehow puzzling. She found that she could think of Michael now with no feeling of loss at all. Perhaps she should be grateful to the ill-mannered Dr Craig for taking her mind off her past troubles and helping her face herself with a more positive attitude.

'Coffee?' He was suddenly there in front of her, holding a cup. 'Do you prefer it white?'

She took the proffered cup. 'Thank you. I like it black after a meal, Dr Craig.'

He sat down in the next chair. 'Make it Andrew, please. It seems a bit crazy to be too formal out here.'

She felt herself blush a little in the dark. 'If you like.' His voice was gentle, as she had noticed it was when he spoke to Lisa.

Lisa came out then, holding her china cup of green

tea. Craig said cheerfully, 'You see, Lisa, I now have an ally. Eve likes coffee too.'

The little Malay girl sat down with a smile and picked up a bamboo fan. It was indeed very hot and stuffy. 'It looks as though it might rain tonight. I hope it will not be much,' she frowned.

'Don't worry about your flight, Lisa. I'll get you through in time.'

'It is very kind of you, but Balik has just phoned. He will come for me at three tomorrow, so there is no need for you to go to any trouble.'

'It is no trouble. You know that.' Eve tried to read his voice, but it was impossible to tell what he was thinking. She couldn't help but feel that there was an understanding between these two.

There was another ring from the telephone. Lisa rose quickly. 'I hope that is not Balik to say he can't make it.' She ran inside, but was out again in an instant. 'Eve, it is for you. Someone called Michael.'

Eve felt her heart almost stop. Why on earth should he ring now, when she had just decided she had completely recovered? She stood up with studied calm and walked inside with no show of eagerness. She picked up the receiver, feeling her heart thump. 'Yes?' she said casually.

'Eve? Is that you? This is Mike.'

'I gathered that.'

'Eve.' He sounded hurt. 'I've just been round to your place. They said you'd left. I had no idea. I was hoping—I thought—well, I wish you hadn't gone. I wanted to talk to you.'

'Talk away.'

'No, I mean about us, Eve. How the hell can I talk intimately from a hundred miles away?'

Eve found herself suddenly very cool and calm. 'You

did have a certain amount of opportunity before I left.'

'Oh, Eve, I was a fool. I miss you around.'

'That's funny,' said Eve, her voice offhand, 'I don't miss you a bit.' And she knew she was right. 'Good night, Michael.'

'No, wait! When are you due back? Can't we meet? Maybe I could drive out and see you sometime? We can't let it all end just like that. I know I behaved badly darling, but I didn't know my own feelings then. I know them now. I knew them as soon as I walked away from that empty room at the nurses' home this evening.'

She could imagine him, the rather boyish figure wandering back across the lawn to the car park where his little red MG was parked. The new consultant anaesthetist. He hardly looked old enough to be a registrar. She had made plans—so many lovely plans before she had arrived. But she knew with a great certainty that Mike was not the one to share them. If he could be so easily swayed by that glamorous secretary, then he could be swayed again. Dear old reliable Eve was bowing out of the race. She said gently, 'Good night, Mike dear.' She heard him speaking again, but she replaced the receiver very softly back on its rest, hearing with a calm satisfaction the quiet click of total separation.

Then she stepped back—and found herself losing her balance, as she collided with the tall figure of Andrew Craig. He must have heard her last words as he walked past her, his bare feet making no sound in the tiled passage. He caught her quickly, his arms firm and strong. Eve knew at that moment why she did not mind the loss of Mike Grant. This was a real man, a man she responded to totally, without knowing quite why. This was a man who did not give his friendship lightly, but once given, it was never broken. And she knew in that split second, as he caught her against him, steadied her and then released her with total impassivity, that she wanted his friendship. She wanted it very much, just as she had wanted to stay in the warm circle of his arms.

'We'll go down to the village at eight-thirty, if that suits you.' He was cool now, totally businesslike. Yes, he had heard her talking to Mike.

'That's fine. Good night, then.' She did not want to go up, but he clearly did not want to talk. She went upstairs and was rewarded by the sound of Andrew's murmured conversation with Lisa, which went on until after she had fallen asleep.

Eve put on the freshly-laundered sarong next morning. It was becoming second nature. She hoped Andrew Craig would not be too scathing about it.

'Good morning.' The dark brown voice came from the veranda. Eve went to the door. The morning sun was fitful today, as grey clouds built up against the sky. The jungle trees glistened, showing that it had rained in the night.

'Good morning, Doct—Andrew.'

She saw his lips turn up into a smile, though he was staring out at the jungle. 'The case notes are on the table. Read them after you've eaten.'

'Yes, of course.' She went back indoors obediently, as though she always obeyed him—though her disobedience about Jacko must be still fresh in his mind.

Andrew followed her in. 'I have seen the child in the ward. I think she would be better at home. There is nothing we can do here that her own family can't do.'

'Very well.' She ought now to mention the blood test she had ordered, but somehow the words did not come. Eve helped herself to cereal and began to eat silently.

Just then, there was an unmistakable volley of shots. They sounded quite close, and Eve found that she had jumped up in apprehension. She put her coffee cup

down, and it rattled in the saucer as her hand trembled.
'Oh, no! What is it, Andrew?'

There was a short silence. He seemed to be waiting for
more shots, his handsome head turned towards the
door. But after that one burst, there was no more. He
crossed the room quickly, sitting down opposite her at
the table. Eve sat, too, glad to take the weight from
trembling knees.

'It is only right that you should know. There are
several gangs roaming about the jungle in this area,' he
said quietly.

'Communists?'

He gave a short laugh. 'Their politics are their own
affair. As far as I can see, they are nothing but bandits
and brigands. They smuggle, they steal, they terrorise
and they extort money.'

Eve waited. Was that it, or was he going to explain
more? She said tentatively, 'They sounded very near
here.'

'Mmm. They were probably trying to frighten Abbas
into paying his protection money.'

'Protection money?'

He nodded. 'We pay as well, Eve. But we don't pay in
money, which they know we do not have. We pay by
giving them free medical treatment.'

'That's dreadful! Why do you give in to them?' she
asked incredulously.

'Why?' He looked at her, his eyes dark with feeling.
'Because I refused once. And the next time I was away,
they burned down the hospital. And there were four
patients inside.'

'Oh, no.' Eve felt bewildered and very frightened.

'Do you still like it here, Eve? You still want to stay? I
won't insist that you keep to your contract if you feel you
can't take it, you know.' His face was very serious now.

He went on quietly, 'But I'd like you to stay—if you will.'

His words twisted in her breast, filling her with a sudden pleasure. The great Andrew Craig was asking her to stay! Coming from him, it was the best compliment he could have paid her. The best compliment she had ever had in her life. 'Yes, I'm not running away,' she answered stoutly. 'So long as you don't ask me not to be just a little bit scared.'

His smile was brief, but genuine. 'I wouldn't ask you that. It isn't possible, I know.' And there was more warmth between them as he indicated the notes on the table. 'There isn't time to look at these now. Let's go down to Dantang before the rain gets any worse.'

It was indeed beginning to rain, but only lightly. They drove down the road to the village, Eve clutching the clipboard he had given her and the three sets of notes for the patients they were to see. She was fascinated to see him at work, when the dour indifference of his usual manner disappeared and he became animated, cheerful and kind.

Eve did not have much to do this morning. As they visited each modest little house, Andrew Craig introduced her and asked her to start the questioning. But it was soon clear that they regarded Dr Craig as their own private friend, and chattered to him instead of to Eve.

The first patient was the man with sprue—a thin, wiry individual with bright black eyes and a dark check sarong round his skinny body. 'Oh yes, Doctor, we know this Sister Carrol, *lah*. This lady she take Mat Abdullah to Jahin, save his life.'

'That's right, Abdul, *baiklah*. So she will ask you some questions—'

'Mat's mother, she very glad, *lah*. She tell us all how

Sister Carrol come running and look all over for Mat . . .'

Andrew quickly took a thermometer from the immaculate pocket of his white shirt, and popped it into Abdul's mouth. 'Shut up for a minute, Abdul. Now— nod or shake your head when I ask you these questions.' There was a twinkle in the blue eyes and an answering one on the swarthy face of his patient. Eve watched, her heart softening towards Andrew by the minute. This was no automaton. The man was full of feeling, and of humour too. The more she watched him with the villagers, the more she thought that they were very fortunate in their medical practitioner.

They made their last call to the boy of twelve, Raman. As they had hoped, there had been no recurrence of his anaemia. He was a smiling, curly-headed lad, slightly made, but active and lively, with no sign of the lassitude and chest pain that would be a sign of returning anaemia. 'He is never still, that boy,' his mother told them, delighted to report the good news. 'But I give him lot of meat, lot of chicken, lot of vegetables.' She was anxious to make it clear how she had obeyed the doctor's instructions.

Andrew examined the lad's chest, and felt with his elegant fingers in his neck for any sign of enlarged glands. 'Just tell Sister Carrol how you have been since I saw you last.'

Eve folded the notes to a clean page and began to ask the routine questions. 'I speak in Malay, Raman, and you must tell me if I say it wrong.' Grinning, showing pure white teeth, the lad obeyed, obligingly speaking more slowly so that Eve was certain of the correct answer. Raman's mother insisted on making a pot of green tea while they worked, and it was welcome after a morning of talking. Eve sipped the tea and put the notes neatly away, while Andrew asked Raman about getting into the school hockey team. The little room was filled with gentle conversation.

Suddenly the bamboo curtain was pulled aside from the front door. The occupants of the room all stared in amazement as the grotesque figure of the Bomoh entered, his eyes ringed with white paint, his naked chest wreathed with the necklace of monkey skulls. 'I hear the witch from the clinic is here.' He grunted the words in Malay.

Andrew rose to his full height, dwarfing the skinny form. 'No, Bomoh, only the doctor and the nurse.' He spoke quietly, but already the aggressive resentment of the Bomoh had turned to cringing cowardice as he recognised the Tuan Doctor. With a snarl almost like that of an animal, he backed and ran from the entrance. Andrew said calmly, 'I think he is a little simple.' He finished his tea. 'Thank you. I will see you in two months, Raman. But come at once if you are worried about anything.'

'I'm glad he came while I was there. I don't believe he is dangerous, but such types can sometimes be trouble-makers. I think I warned him off,' Andrew comforted Eve as they drove back.

She breathed a deep sigh of relief. 'With the Bomoh as well as the gangsters in the bush, I'm beginning to be more of a liability than a help to you.'

'Not a bit.'

'But you are having to stay here just because of me, aren't you?'

He smiled at her briefly as he turned the Rover into the grassy car park. 'Not just because of you. The atmosphere is quieter here for me to catch up on my notes. I was hoping you could give me a hand with them.'

They were walking up to the hospital now, across the

monsoon drain which now had a little rain at the bottom.
'Oh, yes, I'd like that very much.'

'You would?' He smiled down at her and she felt
herself blush, realising that she had perhaps sounded
rather too eager.

'Oh—yes. When Leila goes home, I shall have no
in-patients to look after. It will be good to be busy.'
There, she had explained it. Now he could not possibly
think that she was falling for his good looks, could he?
All the same, they walked up to the veranda and into the
hospital with a warm feeling of comradeship that was far
away from the shame she had felt when his eyes first saw
her, dirty and sweaty at Abbas's garage.

The phone was ringing. Andrew got there first and
answered it. 'Craig here. Oh, yes—tomorrow, if that
would suit you, Edward.' He explained to Eve, with a
hand over the mouthpiece, 'The Palace.' Then he went
on listening. Edward? Was that the Sultan, then? Not a
very Malay name. Andrew was talking. 'One of the
nurses is taking her leave. Yes, the English girl is here.
You would? Certainly. Lunch would be fine. I'll just ask
her.'

Eve had been going away, to wash her hands before
lunch. Andrew called after her. 'Eve, the Sultan would
like to meet you. Lunch tomorrow, if you have no other
engagements.'

The Sultan! Eve smiled. 'Only the hospital.'

'Oh, that will be all right. Anya can telephone the
Palace if we are needed.' And he confirmed the arrange-
ment. Eve was pleased, and a trifle flattered to meet a
Sultan in her first week. And the only thing to spoil
her pleasure was the thought that she had nothing to
wear. She smiled down at her sarong. It would have to
do.

Lunch was always a simple meal, followed by a siesta.

But Anya seemed to think that Lisa had to be built up before her holiday and had piled the gleaming white cloth with pakoras, samosas and curry puffs.

'Oh, Anya, my sister will think I have been doing nothing but eat out here,' Lisa protested. But she did justice to the food, and Eve found herself urged on by the delicious savoury fragrance. Afterwards they lingered, drinking green tea on the veranda. Eve and Andrew did not want to leave Lisa to go off by herself.

The rain was gentle and intermittent, the atmosphere stuffy and very hot. It would have been better to have a downpour, except that Lisa might not get through the jungle roads to Kuala Lumpur. Conversation flagged as they all began to feel sleepy. Andrew said suddenly, 'I think I hear your young man coming, Lisa.'

'He's not that. Oh, how could you?' Lisa was suddenly very confused, and blushed prettily and toyed with her cup.

'I'd like to say goodbye before he arrives.' Eve saw from Andrew's manner that the two men did not see eye to eye. Was it about Lisa? Whatever it was, Andrew stood up suddenly and went inside the hospital. Lisa followed him, so that Eve did not see what kind of farewell they took of each other. She sipped her cold tea and tried not to listen to the murmured conversation inside.

When they came out, Balik's rattling little car had already appeared round the bend from the village. 'So goodbye, my dear. My regards to your family. And let us know how you are.' Andrew was holding both Lisa's hands. Eve turned away quickly, feeling suddenly as though she were prying into their private lives. It shouldn't matter to her whose hand Andrew Craig held. She tried to smile in a welcoming way as Balik parked with a jerk and bounced jauntily across the bridge towards them. By the time he reached the hospital, Andrew had disappeared.

In seconds, Balik's happy disposition had cheered them. The glistening smile in the olive face dimpled, and he bowed low before leaping lightly up the steps. 'It is very kind of you to help me like this, Balik,' Lisa smiled shyly.

'My lovely Lisa, surely you know that I am always glad of an excuse to take a day off—especially with female company of this quality.'

Lisa laughed at his teasing, but Eve thought she detected a look of more than just friendship as Balik looked at the lovely dark-haired nurse. No wonder Andrew did not want to meet him, if they were both in love with the same woman. There was no time for puzzling anything out just then, however, because Balik said that the road further down was becoming quite muddy and slippery. He loaded up Lisa's bags and then held out his hand to her. 'Your chariot, my lady.'

Lisa turned to Eve. It was hard to read the lovely face. Did she mind leaving Andrew alone with Eve? 'Goodbye, Lisa. Have a wonderful time, and don't worry about me. I'll enjoy—' she was going to say, 'taking charge,' but it sounded wrong. She substituted, '—the challenge.' It sounded lame, but there was nothing else she could think of.

Lisa reached out suddenly and squeezed her hand. She smiled briefly. 'Good luck, Eve. I hope it goes well,' Then she took her place in the car and, as the battered vehicle negotiated the bend with the ease that comes from much practice, waved goodbye. Eve lifted her hand, but she saw from the direction of Lisa's face that she was not waving to her, but to the upstairs room where Andrew must be standing.

Did he feel empty, she wondered, as the car taking the

pretty nurse was swallowed up by the dark jungle? She sat down again in deep thought, her chin on her hands. Her pleasure in being the chief nurse, of being the single assistant to a dedicated and interesting man, was overshadowed by the guilty knowledge that it would be wrong if Lisa came back and found that Eve's relationship with Andrew Craig had matured into something more than friendship. Eve had to live out the next three weeks making sure that very thing did not happen. It must not happen, even though she knew that her feelings were becoming more involved with the handsome doctor every second she stayed here.

Through the suffocating afternoon, she heard the phone ring. She had been almost asleep there on the veranda, but she roused herself at the sound. Then the ringing stopped. Anya must have answered. Eve let her head droop again in her hands.

She heard Andrew Craig's voice. He must have come down to the phone. There was a short silence as he listened, then the click as he returned the receiver. She heard his feet padding quietly to the front door, then the sound of him slipping on his sandals, and then he stalked out to where she sat. She looked up at him, expecting to see the face of a friend, and sat up with a start. His brows were beetling in a frown, his attitude stiff with anger. 'You asked for a Paul Bunel test for Leila?' The voice was deep and taut with suppressed feelings.

'Yes, I did.' The short truce was over between them, it appeared.

'Damn it, woman, you know there was no need! The diagnosis is ninety-nine per cent certain. What on earth got into you, to demand an expensive test for nothing? If you go on like this, there'll be no funds for the other hospitals—and what's more, no funds for the tests that we really need to do.'

Eve bristled. 'I had to be sure, sir. I once saw a child die of leukaemia—and the symptoms were just the same.'

'The symptoms are not the same,' he snapped. 'My God, I was here, wasn't I? From now on, do nothing on your own initiative. Do you understand?' He turned sharply on his heel. 'That ruptured spleen you picked up has gone to your head,' he snapped, and he went abruptly inside, swishing the curtain aside and kicking off his shoes angrily. Eve watched him go. Yes—he was missing Lisa. Now she was sure.

CHAPTER SEVEN

WHEN Andrew Craig came down to supper that night, his temper was more under control. Eve was determined not to allow his moodiness to upset her. She was justified in asking for that blood test—yet she knew Andrew was right. She ought to have checked with him first. She was sitting demurely at the table when he appeared, writing a letter to Aunt Marian, her only relative. She looked up and smiled, not expecting any response. To her surprise, he wished her a gruff good evening.

Encouraged, Eve said, 'It was impulsive of me to ask for that test. The ambulance was there, and I felt it would be a waste not to use it.'

He had walked over to the tray, where he mixed them both a drink. He handed her the amber liquid and in a restrained tone, said, 'Maybe I hadn't explained the set-up here properly. It may be my fault. But we only get tests done that are a hundred per cent necessary.'

Eve accepted the glass. 'I'll remember.' She put it down on the table and sealed her letter. 'I said I would drive Leila and her mother home before dinner. I can post my letter at the same time, if you don't mind.'

Andrew frowned a little. 'It's very dark. The sky is cloudy tonight and there are no stars and very little moon. Can't it wait until morning?'

Eve smiled. 'Have you ever been in hospital? That little girl can't wait to get home. I have told her mother to keep her in bed, or at least resting. There won't be any problem because her grandmother will stay with her when her mother goes to work.'

'I'll take her, then.'

Eve shook her head. 'It's all right, Andrew. I'm not afraid.'

'Only fools wouldn't be afraid. Have you forgotten the Bomoh?' he replied rather irritably.

'If it comes to that, what do I do here all alone if the bandits come?' Eve asked pointedly.

'They won't hurt you. They only come if they want medicines. And they don't come inside. They whistle.'

'I know.' But Eve did not insist on taking the child and soon Andrew put down his glass and called Anya to bring Leila and her mother out to his car.

As he was going out of the door he said shortly, 'I'll take your letter down, if you like.' And she gave it to him, feeling as though she was causing him far too much trouble. He certainly had an ability to be ungracious, this man. Yet she had seen his face when he was talking to the villagers, to young Raman and the talkative Abdul. There was a sensitive kindness deep down. Maybe you had to be ill before you could tap his well of smiles and jokes.

Eve watched the rear lights of the Rover as he drove down the path in the drizzle. He was right, of course. It was a nasty night to be out, and especially for a woman. She smiled grimly to herself. That was the second time today that she had admitted to herself that Andrew Craig was right! Oh dear. She knew that very soon she might have to admit to herself that she actually liked the man, and that would be too much—especially when she had resolved not to let herself become any further involved with him.

When he returned, only minutes later, she racked her brains to think of impersonal, harmless conversation. It was all right for a while. She learned that he had graduated from Cambridge and worked for several years in Edinburgh, until he gave in to the charm of the East. But more than that he would not reveal. A secretive man, she was sure that there was more that he preferred not to speak about.

'You don't have to make conversation, you know.'

'What do you mean?' She looked across the table at the blue eyes which were suddenly rather amused in the lean, tanned face.

'I'm quite partial to a companionable silence.'

She wouldn't be squashed. 'So am I sometimes—but not when I want to find out things.'

At that he actually laughed. 'You know, Eve, you are occasionally quite sweet.'

'Are you patronising me, Dr Craig?' She regarded him gravely.

'Quite possibly.' He passed her a dish of saffron rice. She noticed it because it was the first time he had offered it to her before helping himself.

After the meal they had their coffee indoors, in spite of the heat. Somehow it was too gloomy to sit on the veranda and look at the misty jungle through the rain. Eve said casually, 'I miss Lisa.' She sipped her coffee and watched Andrew covertly to see if there was any reaction at the name.

'She needed a break,' was all he said, his face as impassive as any oriental. 'But I must say it seems odd not to have that green tea smell spoiling my coffee.' He was disguising it well, if he had any tender feelings for Lisa.

There was silence. The crickets outside were muted because of the rain. Andrew crossed the room to a small cupboard and took out a couple of cassette tapes. 'What is you taste in music? Let me see if I have anything here that you like.'

'Oh, anything delicate and pretty. I'm not fond of banging and screeching.'

'You mean opera and big symphonies?' He was laughing at her again, and she didn't mind at all. In fact she felt a warmth and a glow as they exchanged simple pleasantries so naturally. 'How about a bit of ballet music?'

'Lovely.' She sat at the table again, after taking their coffee cups to the kitchen. 'And would you like to explain the paperwork you want some help with?'

'Good idea.' He brought down his battered brief-case and showed her some of the tables he was compiling of the incidence of nutritional anaemias in his area. 'Here, you see, I have included a column for social class. They are mainly village people, but Abdul has some training as a civil engineer and there are a couple of school teachers in the next village. So I feel we ought to include this.'

Eve scanned the notes, now all jumbled up and in no sort of order. 'I still don't see how you can complete this kind of work with no histology.'

He smiled. 'You are over-fond of laboratories, I can see. Well, if it will satisfy you, I shall be taking blood samples at the end of next month. I do the whole lot together and drive over to the biochemistry department in KL. They give me half a day to myself. And a couple of good-looking girls to help.' He watched her quizzically. 'Lisa will be back, so you can come with me if you like.'

By the time she went to bed, Eve was feeling decidedly euphoric. After all the animosity of their early relationship, they were suddenly getting to know and like one another. She sighed involuntarily. She must remember her decision. She must not take advantage of Lisa's absence. And if she were truthful to herself, she had not thought there was any danger. This arrogant, attractive, overpowering male was too much his own man to ever allow a mere woman to have any effect on him, unless he chose.

Eve was not to know the confusion in the mind of the man she had already pigeon-holed as aloof, unfeeling, and set in his ways. He had also retired to his room and proceeded to pace the room tirelessly for the next twenty minutes, wondering at the sudden effervescence in his mind, after the calm but boring certainty of the last five years. He almost resented the change. And yet—it was so different. Surely he must not allow himself to be old before his time? And even more disturbing, perhaps he was to be given no choice . . .

Next morning, he was anxious to be off to the Palace. It was still raining, on and off and the weather had kept villagers away from the clinic, so there seemed to be no need to wait around.

'Go and get ready, Eve. No one will come this morning. If they do, Anya will telephone if it is urgent. She knows what to do.'

Eve agreed. 'I'm afraid I have nothing else to wear.'

She watched carefully as Dr Craig looked briefly at her slim-fitting sarong, and allowed his gaze to linger on her fair curls nestling on her neck and shoulders, the slim waist emphasised by the graceful Malay garment. 'You look all right.' It was a curt, almost gruff comment, but Eve was a woman and sensed an approbation belied by the dour words.

He brought the Rover close to the monsoon drain, so that she did not have to get very wet. She looked back at the little hospital as they drove down the jungle road. It was so soon hidden by the rain, the sodden trees, the gloomy undergrowth. Eve wondered what happened at such times to the bandit gangs. Did they have shelter? Did they ever wonder what it must be like to have a settled home, a sound roof overhead?

She looked sideways at her companion, driving with care and experience. The handsome profile caused her heart to miss a beat. For a moment she wondered what he was thinking, and had a tiny glimmer of hope that it might be about her. But the set black line of his thick brows belied any tender thoughts. Eve turned back to watching the mud and slime of the jungle roads.

Jolting and splashing, the Rover surged forward, winding between dripping trees and florid green undergrowth. She could only wonder how he found his way so unerringly, for within ten minutes of leaving Dantang village, the lines of trees had been replaced by a grey stone wall, creeper covered.

'Here we are.'

'That was very quick.'

'We aren't really so far from Jahin, as the crow flies. His Highness has a couple of helicopters, so he never feels isolated.'

'Really?' Eve found herself escorted from the car by a footman with a large umbrella. They were soon in a spacious entrance hall, with a lot of carved white marble and a decorative tiled floor. Two other servants came forward and greeted them with deferential bows. Andrew took off his shoes and Eve followed suit, placing them where he had done, in an ornamental rack.

'My dear chap.' A very English voice greeted them, and the rather portly little man, who came forward with outstretched hand, looked very English himself in baggy grey slacks and a loose, short-sleeved shirt worn outside the trousers. 'Nice of you to come,' he smiled. Andrew introduced Eve. 'Charmed, charmed.' He had a very Malay face, square and sallow, but his accent and

manners were pure English public school. 'I do hope
you are going to be able to stay to lunch, Sister Carrol.'

'You're very kind.' They were ushered into a room
which was bright, in spite of the gloomy weather outside.
It had white walls, with luminous turquoise and blue
mosaic tiles on the floor, and a great quantity of gleaming silver bowls and vases of flowers. On one wall stood
an array of Indonesian mythological figures, carved in a
light wood and lit by concealed lighting.

'Sit down, won't you. Your patient won't be long,
Andrew.' The Sultan went to the door to greet a tiny,
graceful woman, who entered so gently that she looked
as though she might blow away. Her dark hair was
dressed elaborately with three jewelled pins that glit-
tered as she moved, over a fragile porcelain face of
delicate beauty. She was wearing a dark silk trouser suit,
edged with gold satin ribbon.

Andrew took the Sultana's slim hand. She gave him a
smile and bowed her head elegantly. 'This is Sister Eve
Carrol, my assistant at the hospital.' Eve was gratified at
the description. It sounded as though he did appreciate
her after all.

The Sultana smiled again. 'It is a pleasure, Sister
Carrol.' Her accent was not as good as her husband's,
but it tinkled like a silver brook, and her welcome was
genuine. She sat down on a silken couch and motioned
her guests to be seated also, for they had risen to greet
her. 'You know what is wrong with me, Sister Carrol?'

'Wrong?'

'Andrew has not told you? I have mixed collagen
disease.'

Eve gasped. 'Oh, you poor—I'm sorry! I didn't
know.' She felt ashamed. She had thought that Andrew
came here so much just for a social life. Now she realised
why he came. No wonder the Sultan treated his wife so

gently. Andrew was taking his patient's pulse. 'You have seen patients like the Sultana, Eve?'

'Yes, indeed. At St Thomas's.' She did not go on. She didn't know how much insight the little Sultana had into her dangerous condition. She could go on with no symptoms for years, Eve knew. But at any time her body's immune system could go disastrously wrong and attack itself.

The gracious lady seemed quite tranquil. 'I feel a lot happier if I have a regular check-up.' Eve watched her gentle beauty with great pity in her heart. Faith in Andrew would not prevent her fragile little body from destroying itself if it chose. But of course it made sense to see her very often. Any symptoms could then be dealt with immediately. Eve handed Andrew his sphig and stethoscope. At least today their royal patient appeared to be very well, and in good heart. Yet Eve noticed the tips of the slim fingers, decked with delicate gold rings, were turning white, in spite of the warmth of the room. Reynaud's Phenomenon. But the Sultana merely waited until her blood pressure had been checked and then picked up a fur muff and slipped her hands inside.

Andrew pronounced her well, and she beamed. 'Now, I am going to take your assistant away from you, Andrew. We will have coffee in my room. We do not want to hear your talk of golf and fishing.' She rose, straight-backed, and Eve walked close beside her, refraining from holding her arm as she so obviously wished to be independent if she could.

They walked along a glass-roofed corridor, a sort of conservatory, lined with luxuriant orchids in full flower. The raindrops pattered on the roof, sounding like tiny bullets, while the side of the corridor was open to the air, like a colonnade. The garden was beautifully tailored, but almost hidden by the falling rain. The Sultana led

Eve to a small alcove where comfortable cushioned chairs were arranged round a small table on which a little maid was placing a silver tray containing a coffee pot and two transparent china cups. The Sultana gave a small sign with her hand which she drew from the muff, and the maid poured fragrant coffee. 'Thank you. We can manage now, Suki.'

Eve sipped from the exquisite cup and admired the taste and quality of life in the Palace. She refused a glossy sweetmeat from a gold plate. 'Now, Eve, tell me about yourself,' the Sultana asked with interest.

Eve smiled. 'I am beginning to wonder if I really know myself.'

'Why is that?'

Eve hesitated. 'Dr Craig thinks that English women who come out here are either frantic do-gooders, or are running away from something.'

She wondered if the Sultana would probe more deeply, but instead the little lady set down her cup, and said softly, 'And of course, he would be the one to know. Because it applies to English men too.'

Eve had not thought of it that way. 'You don't mean that Andrew—I mean, Dr Craig?'

'Call him Andrew, my dear. He is a special friend. Yes, he was running away, I believe.'

'From a woman?'

'From the memory of a woman. One who let him down badly. Too dedicated to her work. A surgeon, I believe, though he never talks of it. Mr Dalasingam told me.' There was a silence while Eve tried to visualise any woman being able to resist the handsome Dr Craig. He was bad-tempered, that was sure. But perhaps— perhaps that was only after he had been deserted by this woman whom he had trusted and loved . . .

'You are thinking very hard, Eve.'

Eve smiled. 'I'm sorry. I didn't realise that I had anything at all in common with him.'

'You have also been let down?'

'In a different way. I didn't know my own mind. I realised later that I had never loved Michael in the true meaning of the word. I am glad I found out in time.'

'And now? You do know the true meaning of the word?' She was twinkling now, teasing gently. 'Eve, you don't have to tell me. I won't ask your secrets.' But as she bent down, hiding her lovely brown eyes with long lashes as she picked up her coffee cup again, Eve felt that Sultana had almost guessed her secret. And she was glad that there was no more time for embarrassing questions, for Andrew himself came striding along the corridor.

'Zamina, your husband reminds you that you must rest for an hour before luncheon.' He stopped, towering above the two women and holding out a hand to help the Sultana to her feet. She touched a small silver bell and the maid came quickly to help her away.

'Do stay. Please walk in the Palace. There are covered walks. You must show Eve around, Andrew.'

'Yes, I'll do that.' They both remained standing until the Sultana had left. The maid returned to take away the tray, and then they were alone in the flower filled alcove, with a green wall of rain hiding the beauties of the garden.

Eve looked up at Andrew, trying to imagine the woman who had spurned his love for her career. She must have been beautiful, highly talented, yet feminine, even alluring. She may even have been as pretty as Lisa Kai, another dedicated woman, who yet had time to fall in love, to be willing to give her own career a second place to a husband's . . . Eve turned away suddenly, feeling a hurt in her chest, just where her heart was. Yes,

Lisa Kai would be a sweet and suitable companion for Andrew Craig.

He in his turn had stopped staring out at the rain and turned towards Eve, leaning his back against a wooden pillar that was wound around with a sweet-scented creeper. He toyed absently with a scarlet flower until it came off into his hand.

'Shall we walk?' He held out his arm and Eve put her fingers into the crook of his elbow, feeling the hardness of the muscle, the warmth of his skin. She did not see the blue eyes darken at her touch or notice the slight intake of breath as her smooth arm touched his.

He did not move, but stood there, so that she had no choice but to stand also, terribly conscious that he was close. She felt suddenly very disturbed. The strength of his body, the smell of him, his aggressive maleness—Eve knew that this was something that mustn't happen. She dropped his arm suddenly and took a sharp step away, clutching at the creeper round the white-painted pillar, feeling her breath coming irregularly, her shoulders shaking.

He came behind her, so that she felt the warmth of his body without any part of them touching. Slowly he put his hands on her shoulders and turned her round to face him. She looked up, unable to look anywhere else because of the tightness of his grip. She was very conscious of the blueness of his eyes, the intensity in them, the lips that now looked soft and kind, not set and grim, as they usually did. 'Don't go away again.' His voice was dark and gentle.

'You mustn't—we mustn't—' She couldn't keep her voice steady.

'Eve—' At that moment there was a vivid flash of lightning which lit up the entire muddy sky, glittering over the landscaped garden. Then, after a breathless pause, the thunder came, like great rocks being thrown around the heavens by angry giants. It clattered and thumped, like some malevolent force. Eve felt Andrew's arms go round her as she shivered. He held her close so that her cheek was against his chest, and she felt the beating of his heart. 'You're afraid of thunder?'

'No.' She wasn't. It wasn't the thunder that made her tremble.

He moved back slightly, so that he could look into her eyes without letting go. 'No?' His lips turned upwards in a teasing smile. It was transforming his face into the tender, gentle man she had seen when he spoke to the children in the village.

He bent his head towards her, and his lips brushed hers lightly. It was a moment of witchcraft, when her self-control melted away, as though by magic. She felt her senses tingle, her reason, her propriety, her judgment disappear. And as the thunder rumbled around them again his arms tightened, and she felt herself welcome his urgent kiss, respond, return it with equal passion. Her arms encircled his body, clutched at the smooth cotton of his shirt, feeling the taut muscles beneath it. The sound of the storm engulfed them both, and Eve felt herself drowning in some magic whirlpool of emotion and irresistible force.

She had no idea how long they remained like this, encircled with the elements, and with a mutually responding delight. He slowly drew his lips away, kissed her forehead gently, looked into her eyes for a moment, before holding her again so tightly that she could hardly breathe. She heard his breath coming in shuddering gasps that he tried to control. They stood together as though carved from a single tree trunk, together the full length of their bodies, active and vibrant in the electricity of the storm around them, and the storm within them.

They both heard the telephone ring at the same time. Andrew let his arms fall to his sides, yet he did not stand back from her for his feet refused to obey him. Eve put her hands behind her, supporting herself against the creeper-decked pillar, feeling an unsteadiness in her knees and not wanting to trust herself to stand upright just yet. Yet in them both, the professional alertness had come back, the knowledge that the telephone call might be from the hospital.

'Doctor? There is a call from the village. Mr Balik.'

He moved at last, and Eve steadied herself and shook back her hair from her face. 'Why should he ring from the village?' He strode along the corridor and Eve followed him, her coolness rapidly taking the place of her previous blissful ardour. 'Craig here. What is it, Balik?'

'The line is down to the hospital. I went up to see if Sister Carrol was okay. Anya said she was with you.'

'Yes. She's okay. Any other problem?'

'Anya wants you to come back. A man from the village came to the clinic with bad stomach pain. He would not let me touch him. I tried to call an ambulance, but there has been a pile-up on the highway, and there are no ambulances.'

'Stomach pain? Any diarrhoea?'

'No, Doctor. He vomited once.'

Craig frowned. 'Okay. We'd better get back at once. It will probably be enteritis, but it just might be an appendix.'

The Sultan had been standing at the door of his office, listening to Andrew taking the call in the entrance hall. 'Duty calls, eh, old man? Too bad. I was looking forward to a chat. You must both dine with us, to make up for this disappointment.'

'Glad to, any time, Edward. Now, where did I leave my stethoscope?'

'In Zamina's room.' The Sultan opened the door to the chamber they had been in earlier. 'My dear, are you here? Andrew has to go.' There was no answer. He went inside the room, Andrew and Eve close behind him. 'Zamina! Oh, my God, Zamina!' He rushed in and gathered up the little crumpled head of silk and jewels from the middle of the floor. He laid her on the silk couch, while Andrew quickly listened to her heart and carefully took her pulse and temperature. The others looked on, anxiety and pathos on the once jolly face of the Sultan.

'There's nothing obviously wrong, Edward. But we will have to get her to KL. She needs the tests doing, urgently.'

The Sultan nodded. He had been through this before. 'The helicopter is on the pad, Andrew.' He motioned to a footman, who went silently from the room to alert the pilot. 'I am afraid there is urgent business here. Please will you go with her, Andrew?'

'I will, of course.' He turned to Eve, fishing in his pocket for his car keys. 'Here Eve, take the Rover. Get to the hospital and make up your mind whether that fellow has an appendix problem or not. If he has, get him to Jahin. If it is only diarrhoea, keep him in the ward on boiled water, sugar and salt, and I'll get in touch as soon as I can. Right?'

'Right.' Eve had never driven an automatic before, but now was not the time to mention that. She took the keys, while two footmen brought a stretcher that had obviously been used before for the same emergency. The Sultana was laid gently on it and Eve looked down in pity at the transparent skin of the unconscious lady as she was carried out towards the waiting helicopter. She heard the rotors spinning, the sound of the motor revving up, and prayed that the storm would abate in time for this vital journey.

Eve walked out to the Rover. She couldn't see the helicopter, but the noise of its engine was loud and urgent. She heard some shouts as the Sultan gave directions to his pilot and his staff. The rain had eased a little following the thunder, and that was a small mercy which she was glad of as she opened the car door. Getting in, she adjusted the front seat from Andrew's six foot length to her own five foot four. She started the engine. She knew the seven or eight miles back to the plantation hospital would be slippery and dangerous, even in a car that she was used to. But it had to be done, and there was no point in worrying about it. With a murmured prayer, for herself as much as for the Sultana, she pressed the accelerator and eased off the handbrake. The long car purred forward, and then stalled with a little jerk.

'Come on, come on, you can do it.' She found the button for the windscreen wipers, and that improved things a lot. 'Now, have another try. And this time do it properly,' she told herself sternly.

'Eve, Eve!' Someone was calling her. Flustered, she stalled again, and this time the Rover slithered a little before coming to a halt slightly askew.

Andrew Craig was bending down to talk to her through the open window. 'I thought you were in the helicopter!' she exclaimed.

'I just wanted to—to say—' For once she saw him completely careless of his appearance. He stood there in the rain, his wet hair falling over the handsome face, his bare feet muddy, as he had run out without bothering to put his shoes on. His shirt, too, was muddy, and had lost its smart creases of the morning.

She looked out at him as he brushed back the damp lock of hair from his eyes. 'Yes?'

'Be careful.'

She managed a smile. 'Don't worry. I'll take care of your precious Rover.' She switched on, and eased the accelerator again. 'Good luck with Zamina.'

Through the rain his voice reached her as she pulled smoothly away. 'I don't give a damn about the car, lass!'

CHAPTER EIGHT

THE SOUND of Andrew's last words, borne through the wind as Eve drew away from the grey stone wall of the Sultan's Palace, sang in her head as she drove. The driving rain might have terrified her, had she let it. But as she forced the sleek Rover down the muddy road, it was the urgent, passionate way he had jerked out those sweet sentiments, had called her 'lass'. They bore her up as she negotiated slippery bends in the road. They echoed and re-echoed round her brain as she battled with the windscreen wipers and bounced in her seat as great slabs of green water battered against the car.

The road was flooded at Dantang just past Abbas's gas station. But she knew the way now, and knew the water was not too deep to get through. Abbas was in his little cabin and half rose, eyes wide, as Eve pressed the accelerator and whooshed through the flood and on, up to the higher ground that led to the hospital. She did not have a spare hand to wave to him, but somehow she was glad he had seen her, that Abbas knew there was a responsible nurse at the hospital now. It could be important.

The monsoon drain was almost full of muddy water. Eve dashed across the bridge, kicking off her sandals at the door and running inside, her sarong soaked in that brief minute. 'Anya? Are you there?' She didn't stop for an answer. The patient with the abdominal pain—he would be in the ward. She walked swiftly along the corridor, sweeping her wet hair back with her hands, ready, as always, to tackle an emergency with coolness and good judgment.

There were so many other things that mimicked an appendix problem. She must remember the questions to ask. She must not forget anything vital. In these conditions, she might have to take the chap to Jahin herself—and she would look pretty silly if he had only eaten something that disagreed with him last night.

'Anya?' But no one came. The ward was dim and Eve put on the light, glad that at least the electricity had not failed. A man lay on top of one of the white beds, dressed in ragged jeans and a loose shirt. It was hard to tell his age, but he was thin, and lay motionless. That, she thought, was a good sign. At least he was not writhing in pain. 'I'm Sister Carrol. What is the trouble?' She spoke in Malay. There was little response in the dark face. 'You have some pain?'

The man's eyes slithered from side to side and then fixed on her. There was something in them that made Eve shiver and feel herself cold all over, in spite of the sweaty heat of the clammy afternoon. This man was not in pain at all. There was suddenly a triumphant sneer on the dark face. Whatever he wanted, it was not medical attention. Eve stood up straight and backed away a couple of steps, nervously smoothing her damp hair, feeling her spine tingle with a cold fear. 'Anya? Come here at once.'

There was no answer. Eve turned and ran to the kitchen. It was empty. Anya must have gone down to the village to buy food. She had a sister there, and would no doubt stay and have a meal with her. She stopped, waited. There was no sound in the shadowy hospital surrounded as it was by the ceaseless falling rain.

Eve knew she could not bear to go back to the ward. She stood, holding her breath. She was alone. There was no chance of Andrew getting here before evening. She had to face this menacing stranger alone.

She heard a sound. Footsteps. Shuffling footsteps. Whoever he was, he was coming to find her. Eve braced herself, and all her training went into her straight back, her deep breath, her determined stance. With a disturbed personality, she knew she must be the one to show no fear and take the initiative from the start.

When he appeared at the door, Eve was almost relieved. She ought to have realised. In spite of the ragged clothes, the shabby shirt, that skinny body should have been familiar. He stood at the kitchen door, and he had draped the necklace of skulls around his lean torso. It was the Bomoh. And he hated her.

For a long moment they faced each other. Eve breathed deeply, trying to control her panic. 'What on earth do you think you are doing here?' She rapped out the words in her best Hospital Sister English. After all, the English had always been renowned for their stiff upper lip. She knew she must show no fear.

But the Bomoh showed no fear either. He was not a stupid man. It took deep cunning to be able to lure her here, with no suspicion on the part of Anya or of Balik. He had even bluffed Balik about his stomach symptoms. No, the Bomoh was far from stupid. But deranged, now that was possible, and much more dangerous.

He grinned then. His teeth showed, with black spaces, in the flickering shadows, for Eve had not bothered to put on the light. He grinned and rattled the monkey skulls around his neck in a macabre attempt to frighten her. But Eve was no village woman. To her, he was only a man shaking a grisly sort of necklace, though she owned afterwards that the sound had brought her out in goose-pimples. Then he whirled around once, with a weird hollow cry, and leapt away. With an almost sickening sigh of relief, Eve heard him rush through the front door and lurch insanely down the jungle path.

Eve went to the tap and drew herself a long drink of water unmindful of the fact that usually they never drank water straight from the tap, as it was always too warm. Anya made sure there were three or four bottles of cool water in the fridge. But this was different. On this occasion Eve, though knowing that she was no longer at the mercy of that Bomoh, had to sit down and drink in order to calm herself down.

Her heart rate gradually returned to normal. Eve knew she ought not to long for Andrew Craig. After all, she had promised herself that she would manage alone, show them how well she could take charge. But she found herself hoping for him to show up.

She went along the corridor. She would go upstairs and change her crumpled sarong, wash her face and shake off the feelings of menace and fear. She still wished she were not alone, but at least the Bomoh had gone and she would be able to secure the doors against any further problems.

It was getting dark. The day had never been bright, but now the evening was setting in and the sky was lowering over the dark, drenched trees. Eve walked along the corridor and put the lights on in the sitting-room. It was lonely, empty without either Lisa or Andrew Craig. But at least it was familiar, and Eve knew that Anya would return shortly with vegetables and meat for the next few days.

Then she drew in her breath in a great sobbing gasp. There, hanging from the ceiling, was a dangling, floppy doll. It was made of cloth, with yellow cotton for hair. And in its little body were jabbed six or seven long pins. It was a witchcraft doll, and the pins were clearly meant to show Eve that she had been condemned by the

Bomoh. Even though she knew it was rubbish, and she had never believed in such superstition, Eve sobbed in sudden despair that she could be so hated when she had only come here to do her best to help.

She crouched for a moment, hurt by the thought. But it was not in her nature to allow life to get the better of her, and she soon stood up, tall and confident. She looked up at the string holding the doll. It was stuck with a scrap of plasticine. In a second, she had reached up and knocked the whole thing to the ground. At the movement, the seven green lizards on the ceiling scuttered frantically to the corners, terrified by the noise.

'It's all right, my friends. The evil one has gone away.' Eve murmured the words gently as she gathered the model and wrapped it firmly in an old piece of newspaper. She was not going to allow this silly incident to have any effect on her.

There was a loud noise outside. Eve's nerves were so stretched that it did not register with her. All she knew was that she was standing alone, her heart thumping with the effort to stay calm, and then suddenly the curtain at the door was brushed aside, and Andrew Craig stood there, his dark eyes wide with concern.

'Eve? Are you all right?' He was at her side in two strides.

She turned to him, ready to explain what had happened, and how she had coped. But somehow the words didn't come, and she found herself holding back hot tears, as she said 'Andrew! Oh, Andrew, thank God!'

Then he was holding her, and she could contain the tears no longer. 'It's all right, my lass. It's all right. I'm here.' She knew it was Andrew's voice, but never had she heard it so tender, so raw with feeling.

This was the man who had taken great care to show how much he objected to her dress, to her independent attitude. And now she was in his arms, not wanting to be anywhere else in the world, and his lips were against her forehead, and his murmured words felt by her beating heart.

Andrew found the doll without being told. 'The Bomoh. You mean to say this was the patient? My God, what a sick mind he must have!' He gathered up the figurine, wrapped it again in the newspaper that Eve had used, and marched out to the back of the hospital with it. When he returned, Eve had controlled herself. She thanked him formally. They were no longer close.

'I'm glad to see you.' She said the words, but no longer did they have the spontaneity of her first enraptured cries.

'Did he do anything? Was he violent?' Andrew's concern was still very obvious. 'I thought you might have trouble from the gang in the jungle—but this maniac! I never imagined for a moment—'

'It—it is over, Andrew. I don't think he could hurt me, not physically. Now that I've faced him I know he won't bother me again.'

'Maybe you're right.'

There was a silence. They both stood in that shadowy room and Eve longed with all her being to hear him call her 'my lass' and feel his powerful, almost cruel arms around her, defending her from the world. But now that she was no longer terrified she was using her head, not her heart, and she knew that Lisa was away, and she had promised herself she must never take advantage of that. It was even more wrong, now that she knew how bitterly Andrew had been disappointed. Eve was now sure that Lisa Kai had been well on the way to healing Andrew's hurt. It was wrong and selfish of her to interfere just because Lisa was on holiday. Let her come back—there would be no danger, then, of Andrew taking consolation in his new nurse just because she was the nearest loving presence . . . Loving? As Eve lowered her gaze, she knew beyond doubt that Andrew Craig was rapidly assuming the primary place in her life. It had to stop. This was wrong. She must prevent it at all costs, before she said anything she would regret.

Fortunately, she thought of a question. 'How did you get here so quickly? How is Zamina?'

He beckoned her to accompany him to the front room. There, he took out the Martini and the other mysterious bottles from which he made his usual evening cocktail. While he worked, he said, 'She is well. It might have been a simple faint. But I have asked the team in KL who are looking after her to do all the tests again.'

'Heart tests, liver function, kidney function—'

'I saw you notice her Reynaud's Phenomenon.'

'Oh, Andrew, she is such a wonderful lady—'

He looked down at her as he held out a drink. 'She is, of course. And Selim—Edward—is one of my closest friends. But remember, Eve, this disease was unknown until this decade. That means that many people who suffer from it have no symptoms at all, or only minor ones—'

'Like recurring temperature? Joint pains?'

Andrew sat down beside her, stretching his long legs in front of him and sipping his Martini. 'Oh, Eve, yes. You don't have to show me any more. I have a treasure on my staff, someone who knows her medicine backwards.' She turned to him with a smile. 'I apologise for ever doubting your ability, just because you wore a sarong. I was wrong, and very rude,' he admitted.

Eve felt again that she was being disloyal to Lisa. 'Tell me about Zamina.'

'I have hopes, lass, that she might never get worse.'

'Oh, yes, so have I.' And as Andrew held up his glass, Eve responded. Then she noticed something. 'There's no noise. Can that rain actually have stopped?'

'I think you're right.' Andrew unwound his long limbs and Eve tried not to notice his healthy litheness, his muscular perfection as he stood up, and strode to the veranda. 'Come out, Eve! Look at the stars.'

She longed to. But she stayed where she was, sitting at the table. 'If we both look at the stars, then neither of us will eat tonight. Anya isn't here.'

He came in and his handsome face was smiling and relaxed. 'Don't worry. I'm very good at chapatis.' It was so hard not to respond to his easy, relaxed attitude. Yet all the time, Eve was thinking that she was being a heel, intruding into a relationship that was just becoming established. Lisa would be good for Andrew, there was no doubt of that. Lisa obeyed his every edict and knew that everything he said was right. And it was so wrong for her to be here with him, alone in the jungle. Her own feelings were now so plain to her, that Eve knew clearly she would fall into his arms if he merely said the word. It was an uncomfortable knowledge, and one that prevented her from enjoying watching Andrew Craig as he rolled out the dough and threw the chapatis into the wok, one at a time.

As he worked, Andrew said idly, 'This Mike of yours. Someone who means a lot?'

Eve felt her heart miss a beat. He had been listening that night. But it was a good opportunity to put a stop to this easy familiarity. She was certain that he was only being pleasant because they were marooned together in the storm. Now, she had the chance to stop him. She had to—even though she knew in her own heart that her own feelings had been affected by an irrefutable force. 'Mike? You heard me talking to him?'

'I'm afraid I did. Life in Dantang isn't terribly private. You must have noticed.'

'I did, Andrew.' She looked at him, loving him. Then she swallowed and turned away. She said, and it wasn't a lie, 'I came out to Malaysia to marry him.'

There was a long pause. Andrew Craig put the last of the chapatis on the plate. Then he dried his hands on a towel. 'We can't have these by themselves.' And he quickly set about pouring lentils into a pan and covering them with spices and water. 'Slice some of that ginger into there, Eve, would you?' He was impassive. He was not bothered one bit by what she had said. That was good. Eve didn't want any problems. It was clear now that there wouldn't be any.

She did as she was told, cutting the fibrous root so that delicate aromas drifted round the little room. Andrew had meanwhile sliced an onion into the wok, and it was simmering gently. He took the ginger from her and deftly mixed it with the onions, with other spices, before adding the lentils. She could not help smiling in admiration. 'You do it awfully well.'

He glanced at her and nodded drily. 'I'm glad you find me some use about the house.'

'I didn't mean to be rude.' Confused, she tried to justify her comments, only to find him shaking his head in amused exasperation. 'I'm sorry.'

'Don't bother being sorry. Just tell me what you would have eaten if I hadn't been here?'

She thought for a moment. 'To be very honest, I'd have made some black coffee and picked some bananas.' Eve pursed her lips. 'I say, I'm rather useless, aren't I?'

'Not really—I'm sure you'll know how to make dhal next time. You were watching me, weren't you?'

'Yes—but I didn't spot which of those spices you used. And all the containers look the same to me.'

Craig gave a final stir to the lentils, and put the lid on. 'Come on. One more Martini, and it will be ready.' He led the way through to the front room. As he poured the drinks, he said, 'Maybe when you have finished putting my notes in order for me, I'll give you a couple of cookery lessons. At least it will take your mind off that Mike of yours.'

Eve took the drink, conscious that her cheeks were reddening. How she wished she could tell him the truth—that when he had heard her saying goodbye to Mike, it was the last time she would ever speak to him. But she held the information back. If Andrew believed her to be engaged, he was not likely to forget his own attachment to Lisa. And Eve had no intention of being the 'other woman' to come between them while Lisa was away. It would be sweet, achingly sweet, while it lasted. But she knew she would only hate herself if she let herself do anything so underhand to Lisa.

'You didn't answer me.'

Eve took a careful sip of her Martini and said, trying to keep her voice quite matter of fact, 'You didn't ask me a question.' And she realised that he had moved closer to her and was standing within touching distance. Her heart began thumping as the male scent of him came to her, recalling the kiss, the unexpected passion that the storm had roused in them. For those few moments, he had made the rest of the world disappear.

He said in a low voice, 'I understand. You don't want to talk about your Mike. Fair enough. I can take a hint.' For another few seconds they stood motionless. She knew she could have broken the silence with the truth. But she dare not. The shadow of innocent Lisa hovered between them, and Eve stayed silent. Craig suddenly turned on his heel, tossed off the rest of his Martini, and strode from the room, saying as he went, 'Dinner is served.' Eve knew he was trying to be casual—and she knew he did not succeed. He was too honest, too sincere a man to show feelings that he did not feel.

They ate the food almost in silence. After some time, Andrew said lightly, 'Mr Balik must think quite a lot of you, Eve. You do know that he had driven up here in the rain, just to make sure you were all right?'

'He had?' Eve looked up from her plate. She saw the intense blue eyes piercing into her soul, trying to read her innermost thoughts. She smiled. 'I don't think so. He probably wanted to sell us some more supplies while he was in the area.'

'I'm not sure that I'd believe that. I'm not convinced that he can be trusted.'

'Oh, Andrew.' Eve was provoked into a response. She recalled the way Andrew had avoided Balik when he called for Lisa. His rival, then. But she wouldn't let Andrew get away with that remark. 'He's an attractive guy, and he's kind. The very first time I met him he got me out of the village so that the Bomoh wouldn't see me. I think you just don't know him very well.'

Andrew nodded slowly and pushed his plate away. 'And maybe I don't want to.' He looked up at her, the blueness of his eyes sharp and compelling.

Eve stood up and took the plates to the kitchen. Her heart was behaving very strangely and she took some deep breaths to steady herself, giving herself a private lesson on the medical causes for palpitations. Adrenalin, she mused—and then blushed hotly, as she realised it was the female hormones responding to the closeness of an attractive male. She plunged the plates into the sink and rattled them about as she splashed them with water, and scrubbed the wok unnecessarily hard with the pan scrubber, until the hotness in her face had ebbed away.

Then she felt composed enough to return to Andrew,

ready to tell him that she was going to shower and have an early night. He was not in the room, but the kettle was still steaming gently, and there was a fragrance of coffee. She went towards the door and drew the muslin curtain to one side. Andrew was sitting, his long legs crossed comfortably, in one of the bamboo chairs. Two coffee cups stood on the table beside him, and two large brandy glasses, with a swirl of amber liquid at the bottom. He looked up and waved an elegant hand. 'Sit down, Eve.'

She obeyed, sitting on the edge of the chair. 'I don't want any brandy, thank you. It gives me hiccups.'

He lifted a black eyebrow. 'Oh, but I insist. Purely medicinal, this time. Anyone would need it after the kind of day you have had.' And he shifted in his chair then, and she saw that the easy pose had only been a front he could not sustain. 'Eve, I've got to say it. You've been marvellous, bloody marvellous. I—may have said some blunt things to you when we first met. Well, I am equally blunt when there's something good to say. I don't know—'

Eve was swift to interrupt. 'Don't. Please don't. It was part of that job that I'm paid to do, and anyone else would have done the same.'

'Perhaps they would, lass. But by now they would have been either hysterical or asleep. And you walk out here as though you have just put down a good book.'

She looked out over the sodden grass to the darkness of the trees beyond. The solid black of the clouds was breaking up and there were streaks of light, where patches of stars glistened through. She felt tears start at the back of her eyes. If only he knew the typhoon that was going on inside her. And to hear that velvet voice praising her, calling her 'lass'—Andrew Craig was nearer to getting his hysterical outburst than he knew.

She breathed in deeply. 'I believe the rain has finally finished.'

She stood up and walked to the railing, knowing that she had failed to keep her voice steady. If only he would leave her alone for just a couple of minutes, she would be able to regain her famous ice-cool calm and to face him again. But now those tears were perilously close to falling, and she had to keep her face averted, gazing out towards the jungle, where the sweet scents of the flowers and leaves were accentuated after the rain.

'Eve, look at me.' Through her own distress, she was conscious that Andrew's voice was trembling too. Anxiously, she turned. He was standing up. It was too dark to read his face, but she could feel the tension between them, the desperate attraction that she knew she had to resist. She could hear the cicadas starting up their song, celebrating the end of the rain. She could see the silver drops falling from the curved eaves of the veranda, sliding down the orchids and into the lush grass below. And she heard his voice, almost as in a dream. 'Come to me?'

For another second, they were still. Then she saw his hands turn palms upwards in the twilight, as though reaching out to her. And though she meant to run past him, upstairs to her own room, she knew she could not. Straight to him she went, knowing that he had come most of the way himself, and they were clinging together as though to life itself. He did not kiss her. He said nothing. But his arms clung to her as though she were the most precious thing in the world, his fingers meshed in her hair, stroking her shoulders, leaning his cheek against her head, his breath coming in shuddering gasps.

She had known it would be sweet. For long moments she allowed herself to be cherished in Andrew's arms, feeling a strange mixture of peace and turbulence slowly overwhelm her. She felt his strong body in her arms, moved her hands along his spine, up to the waving curls on his neck, wondering how a human being could become so precious, so beautiful, so necessary to her own happiness. But even as she felt these unformed thoughts in her mind, other feelings of guilt and wrongdoing flooded in. How would she feel when Lisa came back? What would she say?

Her body stiffened. Andrew sensed it and drew back a little, without taking his arms away. 'What is it?' His whisper was as sensual as his embrace. But Eve was summoning all her resistance. Lisa's trusting face swam before her, china-smooth and pretty, and she saw the deep affection for Andrew she had first noticed in those limpid, silk-fringed eyes.

'Let me go. Please.'

He released her without standing back, his eyes dark and unreadable. 'I am sorry. I didn't think—' He also must be remembering the woman he really loved. His breathing was still irregular but he turned half away, and she knew he also was ashamed at letting such feelings get the better of him. He moved away suddenly, and picked up the two glasses, handing one to Eve. 'Here, Sister Carrol. Give yourself hiccups.'

For a moment, their eyes met. He lifted the glass to his lips, after first raising it to her just a fraction. Eve felt as though her heart would shatter. She dropped the glass and dashed indoors, leaving the curtain swinging.

CHAPTER NINE

WITH THE return of the sunshine next day, Eve was up early, struck with pleasure at the luminous beauty of the shimmering jungle under the clear blue sky that the wisps of mist were deserting like spirits. She had breakfasted alone, glad that Andrew was not yet down. She could only hope that with the welcome normality of the growing queue under the banana trees, the events of the last two days could evaporate with the mist, and never be thought of again.

'Back to normal, Anya.'

'Yes, that is good, missy. The telephone man, already he come and repair the line.' Anya cleared Eve's plate and coffee cup. Eve went indoors to brush her teeth and then took her place in the chair in the shade of the trees. She smiled at the villagers.

'Who is first?'

The surgery proceeded normally. Eve made careful notes of each case and gave out advice or treatment. One young woman thought she was pregnant. Eve made a note to refer her to the visiting midwife—or birth attendant, as she preferred to be called. It would have been nice to take on the village obstetrics too, but the 'baby round' was jealously guarded by the team from Jahin who had done it for ten years now. Eve smiled her congratulations as she told the girl to eat sensibly and wait for the visit of her colleague.

That evening, Eve sat nervously, twisting her fingers together, as she waited for dinner, knowing that she and Andrew would be tête-à-tête for the next two weeks.

She tried to think of subjects of conversation that had nothing personal about them. She must treat Andrew Craig only as a colleague and friend. But the more she worried, the less could she think of anything to say to him. And as the smell of satay grew more delicious and she knew dinner was almost ready, Eve found herself without an appetite, almost deciding to give the meal a miss.

'Eve, I was wondering—could you manage without me for a day or two?' Andrew Craig was at the door, tall, impassive. He entered with his usual grace, the long limbs naturally lithe and elegant.

With a tiny air of relief, Eve said, 'Oh yes, I should think so.'

Craig was mixing his usual cocktail and spoke with his back to her. 'I must visit the other hospitals. And there is a village near Kuanang where I have two patients in my anaemia study. They have to be seen in the next week, so I thought I would get it all done in one trip.'

'That seems a good idea.' She was more relaxed now. She found she was able to look into his face without feeling the force of those piercing eyes. She said, genuinely interested, 'The other village is like Dantang?'

Craig brought her a drink. She could have cried with pleasure that he did not look at her as he gave her the glass, but handed it over as though to a visiting guest, polite but without any formality. And she knew he must be regretting his openness with her, his brief passionate encounter that must have meant nothing to him. He belonged to Lisa, that was sure. He had been deeply hurt, and Lisa Kai had been the woman who had slowly begun to show him that women were not all wilful and selfish. Andrew said, as he folded his long limbs into a chair, 'No, there is no other village quite like this one, with a longstanding father-figure—in the shape of the plantation.'

'I understand. Dantang has been rather like a family, protected by the plantation owner,' Eve nodded.

'Yes indeed. Protected—for his own good, of course. Healthy workers make healthy profits.'

Eve could not have been more grateful. Andrew Craig had brought his own conversation and she did not have to worry. Their conversation flowed as easily as though there had never been anything physical between them at all. And tomorrow he would be leaving for a while. Eve sighed a sigh of relief. The time she had dreaded, the time alone, without Lisa, would pass easily and peacefully if tonight was any guide.

She went up early, with a friendly 'Good night' from Andrew Craig. It was reassuring that there was to be no more pretence between them; that he knew as well as she did that they must be honourable in Lisa's absence. Eve pulled off her sarong and laid it on the chair. She smiled as she looked at it. The village dress that had caused such anger from her boss . . . He seemed not even to notice it now. She slipped her arms into her wispy cotton housecoat and sat for a moment on the bed, staring into space. She heard the crickets outside and the lizards on the ceiling, scuttering on gentle claws in the flickering light of the moon through the window grille.

Eve started. What time was it? She must have been dreaming, for there were unmistakable sounds of Andrew going to his room. And even as she tried to forget him and settle to sleep, she found the image of him holding out his arms to her swimming into her mind. 'Come to me,' he had said. And the words went on and on in her mind. She heard the very catch in his voice, saw the appealing anguish in the outstretched arms. Over and over again she heard the words, 'Come to me. Come to me.' It was almost as though he were saying it now. Eve stood up, the gown swishing around her in the draught from the fan. She even went to the door and opened it a fraction.

Reality caught her, and she pushed the door closed with a little slam. How could she be so foolish? She caught her breath and told herself firmly to pull herself together.

There was a tap on the door and she drew in her breath audibly. 'Who is it?'

The door was opened a crack and Andrew Craig, dressed only in jeans, stood there, framed by the shadows of the corridor and the shaft of moonlight from the bathroom window. 'Are you all right? I heard a bang.'

He must have been as alert as she was to be there so quickly. Eve drew back, knowing that he must not stay here; that any further contact between them must be distant and formal. 'Please go. I'm fine. Go now.' She was conscious that her flimsy gown was falling open, and she pulled the edges together at her neck, feeling her hands tremble as she did so.

'Yes. Sure. Good night, Eve.' And the broad back caught the light as he returned to his room. Eve closed her door and threw herself on to the bed, face down. How could he do this to her? The torture of seeing him there, so close and yet too far for her to bridge the gap—surely she could not go on, bearing it without a word, without a protest? But such was the emotional strain that, even as she lay there, her head buried in her arms, blessed sleep came, and peaceful night soothed her taut agonies and smoothed her cares away.

Composed and sensible next morning, Eve prepared to take the clinic, the emotional state of the previous night seemingly far away and unreal, the ghost of the man she loved only a distant and fragmented dream. She was already questioning her second patient when she heard Andrew's steps on the veranda.

'Sister Carrol?'

'Excuse me.' Eve left her desk and went up to Andrew. He was dressed in his neat short-sleeved shirt and fawn slim-fitting trousers, and his dark hair waved down the strong neck, an unruly lock escaping over the tanned brow, so that he had to shake it back. Eve tried to tell herself that his appearance had nothing at all to do with her job here. She looked up into the lean face, her sensations strictly under control. 'Don't worry, Andrew. I know what to do. And I have the list of phone numbers so that I can get in touch with you if necessary.'

'Good.' He came down the steps of the veranda to the dry grass of the clearing where Eve stood. He lowered his voice. 'Any trouble at all from the jungle, any whistle, anything at all—ring me at once. Is that clear?'

'Of course.'

'And I'll telephone each night. Just for my own peace of mind.' He looked into her eyes then, but Eve refused to meet the gaze. 'I'll want to know if you have any news from the Palace. Zamina will be coming home soon, and she will expect a visit from me.'

'I'll let you know, of course.'

There was nothing else to say. The sun blazed down into the clearing as Eve and Andrew Craig exchanged nods and brief goodbyes. Then she went back to her patient, not turning her head to watch as the dark Rover wound its way down the jungle path. All the same, she listened with her heart, her feelings winding down that path with him, past the gas station and out towards the main highway, until the roar of the Rover had faded to nothing amidst the bustle and flutter of the jungle noises.

'And I have such bad pain in the night, Sister.' It was

the last patient of the morning, and Eve had concentrated well. Although she was sad that Andrew had gone, another side of her was pleased to be allowed to take full charge of the hospital. Now she would be able to start her own routine. Now, at last, she could introduce just the right amount of reform that Dantang needed, without changing its character, without spoiling its informal atmosphere.

'Where is the pain?' Eve waited while the slim, rather anxious-looking woman showed her which part of her abdomen had been troubling her. She smiled to herself, knowing that with such symptoms in Kuala Lumpur, the woman would be sent for an immediate barium meal. 'Ah, yes. And is there anything that relieves the pain?'

'Nothing. Only when I sit up.'

'Ah.' Oesophagitis, maybe. Some of these ladies liked a lot of chilli in their food. 'Does milk help?'

'I do not know.'

Eve explained about the possibility of an inflamed alimentary tract, and advised milder curries for a week or so. It was only as the woman was thanking her that she noticed the dress she was wearing. It was a simple cotton, but very like one that Eve used to have. 'Your dress is pretty, Leena.'

'Is new, Sister. Old Haria sell them in the village, plenty cheap.'

'In the village? Today?' Eve's heart lifted. It *was* her dress. Her suitcase had been found, and her clothes were being sold off! As soon as she could, she walked briskly off down to Dantang village. This was something she must investigate.

And there, at one of the usual wayside stalls, Haria had draped, along with her lengths of batik, the remains of Eve's dresses and one rather crumpled Sister's uniform. The watch was missing from the front, and the silver-buckled belt. But there was no doubt that Eve had found her belongings—and rather too late to do any good, for the only things left were two cheap skirts and the uniform.

'These clothes are mine, Haria.'

The wrinkled face looked doubtful at first, then angry, and then rather fearful. Eve hastened to reassure her. 'I don't want the others. But I would like my nurse's uniform back—and I very much want to know where you got them from.'

She shook her old head, the thin grey hair waving around the little brown skull. 'I do not know. My son—he brings things, many times.'

'Your son?' But Eve saw that the woman was frightened and did not want to upset her. 'Never mind. It doesn't matter. Just give me my uniform.'

The woman handed it over with a sort of sullen haste. Eve felt almost mean for taking it without payment, for she knew old Haria was poor. 'Thank you. *Terimasakih*. I'm glad to get it back.' And she went off quickly, to make it clear she was not going to ask any more questions.

Eve stood in the dirt road, which was edged with palm trees. There were two other stalls at the roadside among the long grass, selling fruit and vegetables. She folded the uniform as neatly as she could and turned to make her way back up the path. But there was a murmuring of voices ahead and Eve noticed a group of villagers standing around a central figure. She knew, without looking, who it must be. The Bomoh. And this time he stood together with old Haria, their heads close together, and the women around them were muttering and gesticulating. Eve knew they were speaking about her. She held her head high and proceeded to walk past the group, trying to still the thumping of her heart. Three small children were playing a game in the dusty soil. One of the women screeched something in Malay and the children stared at Eve with wide brown eyes, and then scuttled away as though she were infectious.

Eve retraced her steps to the hospital, her initial pleasure in the day dashed. Even though she knew the Bomoh to be deranged, it was still hurtful to know that she was feared when she had come here to help the people. Old Haria had never been so resentful before. Was it perhaps that her son was one of the thieves who had stolen her suitcase? The villagers perhaps knew more about the local brigands than they pretended to.

Anya was waiting, a light meal on the spotless cloth. 'Ah, missy, the uniform. I wash it, no?'

Eve handed it over. 'Thank you, Anya.'

Zaina said, tossing back her bushy tail of black hair, 'I thought many of the women were wearing dresses. They were yours?'

'Yes.' Eve sat at the table with her and nibbled at some celery without any appetite. 'Obviously the case has been handed over to Haria to dispose of. It doesn't matter. I don't want the things now.' She would not take them if they were returned. The whole affair was upsetting and she wanted to forget it. 'I will wear Lisa's sarongs until they wear out. Then will be the time to buy more dresses.'

'Doctor will be pleased you have the uniform, Eve.'

'I hope so. Even without the belt, I suppose it does look more businesslike and professional.'

Anya put a plate of thin soup before her. 'If I have the pain in the belly, I do not care if you wear a nightgown, so long as you make me better, *lah*.' She was gentle, and Eve knew she was trying, in her own nice little way, to make her feel the whole thing was nothing to worry about.

'Thank you, Anya. As usual, you are the wisest of the lot of us.'

Dinner that night, and the following two nights, was a lonely affair. Eve had expected to feel relaxed, knowing that the disturbing Dr Craig was not going to be around. But the place seemed very empty without him. Even when he was silent, she had been strangely comforted and secure at his dour, long-legged presence. But she had work to do, for she had admitted two patients to the ward and taken the opportunity to initiate Anya and Zaina to the regular hours that she had been used to at Kuala Lumpur.

'The patients must know when we are coming round to see them. And please, all temperatures and blood pressures to be done first thing, whether you think they need it or not.'

Zaina had not minded the change in routine. 'And when you wear your uniform, you will look very grand and important,' she grinned. They were doing the evening round, before Zaina went home and Anya took charge, sleeping in the small bed in the alcove whenever there were patients.

'I'll wear it tomorrow morning,' Eve replied with a smile. She bent over the first bed. 'How are you feeling now?' She put her hand gently to the forehead of the youth she had admitted with a very high temperature. 'Have you any other pain? Throat? Stomach?'

The lad shook his head. 'No pain, miss. Only feel so hot, *lah*.' Eve took his temperature again. 'It is down a little. Wash him down, Zaina, before you go, and make him comfortable for the night.'

'What is matter with me, miss?'

'I can't tell at the moment. Dr Craig will be back tomorrow, and if you are still like this, he may take you to Jahin. Don't worry, Misra, we will look after you.'

The boy nodded and lay back on the pillows. Eve was hoping that his fever would subside without further treatment, but she left some soluble aspirin to help him settle. She turned to the bed in the corner, where there was no doubt at all about the diagnosis. A ten-year old lad lay with a grin on his brown face, his teeth showing white in the dim light. 'And how are you, my bright spark? How is that foot of yours?'

'Very good, Sister.' The smile did not diminish as she took the bandage from the inflamed foot and examined it closely. 'You going to give me another needle?'

Eve could not help grinning back at him. 'Well, Danny, I've never known anyone so delighted to be in hospital. Anyone would think you trod on that thorn on purpose.'

'Oh no, not on purpose.' He wiggled the toes as she examined them, and for the first time there was a small wince of pain.

'Well, you don't need any more needles. Just take the tablets Nurse gives you before you go to sleep. And no getting out of bed without permission. That little foot of yours wants some rest to get well.'

She wished them good night and stood for a moment talking to Anya and Zaina. Anya said, 'Danny is one of twelve. I think he is enjoying being noticed for once, instead of always being swamped by his brothers and sisters.'

Eve smiled. 'You may well be right.' They looked back at the shadowy ward, where the child was lying like a little king, arms behind his head, bandaged foot stuck out importantly.

Morning dawned bright again. Eve got out of bed, trying not to let her heart leap at the thought that today Andrew Craig was coming back. The uniform helped. She washed herself briskly and brushed back the fair curls into a tidy pleat. Then she took the dark blue dress, now freshly laundered, and held it against her. Yes, she would find it useful, it would give her a sense of being at work. Eve put it on and smoothed it down. It fitted well, even without the belt, and felt cool and crisp. With a final glance at her neat hair and healthy, blue-eyed face, she ran lightly down to breakfast, feeling totally relaxed and fully in control. What a good thing that she had already reorganised the hospital routine to suit her own ideas.

Anya gave her a cup of green tea. 'You look good, missy. Very smart, very strict, *lah*.'

Eve laughed. 'Well, I'm not a slave driver. But it is my policy to see the patients before I have my own breakfast.'

Anya shrugged. 'Okay, *lah*, but I already gave them food and also I do the temperatures for you.' She spoke as they both entered the ward, which smelt of disinfectant and cleanliness. It did not take long to greet the two boys and make sure they had spent a good night.

Zaina was prompt. She too admired Eve's new appearance, and suggested that perhaps she could have a white overall also. They were all joking and light-hearted, but Eve carefully made sure that her new rules were adhered to. She left Zaina taking the blood pressures and handing out the medicines. Eve's heart was light. She was in charge, and her methods were working. She knew that Andrew Craig could find no fault with her now, neither in her dress nor her running of the ward. And she faced his arrival with calmness.

There was only a handful of patients that morning. She had seen them all by eleven and was sitting on the veranda sipping coffee when she saw an unfamiliar figure trudging up the path in the heat. At least—at first he was unfamiliar, until the sun glinted on that reddish-brown hair that she had once thought the most precious in the world. 'Oh no! Mike! I don't want Mike here,' she muttered. She put her cup down and stood up as the sweating young man reached her and crossed the drain to stand looking up into her face.

'Hi, Eve. Don't look at me like that, darling. I couldn't let another day go by without seeing you. We've got to talk.' He was wearing a thin tee-shirt and light blue jeans. He looked more like a schoolboy than a consultant anaesthetist, as he wiped his face with a handkerchief, and put one foot on the step.

But Eve was not moved by his boyish good looks any more. He was too handsome for his own good, and his vanity was enough to ensure that he made the most of the young nurses and secretaries who chased him wherever he worked. 'You shouldn't have come. I did tell you.'

Mike knew how to use his charm. He looked into her eyes, with what she used to call his 'Oliver Twist' look, and said gently, 'You won't even ask me to sit down, love? After I've come all this way?'

'How did you come?'

'In the MG. I left it at that greasy little garage to be washed. He told me it wasn't far.'

Eve said reluctantly. 'Sit down, then. I'll get you a cold drink.'

'Thanks, love.' He took the fresh orange juice from her and tossed it down with relish. 'Now look, Eve, we've both been hasty, and I've been damn stupid, I know. But can we talk about us? *Please?*'

He was pleading, he was dashing, he was very good-looking. But he might as well have been a Martian, for all the effect it had on Eve. She regarded him very gravely.

'In a way I'm glad to see you. It proves to me that I was

right to leave. I really have nothing else to say to you, Mike. We are two very different people now.' She stood up and moved away, looking out at the familiar jungle with its squeaks and bird calls in its lush green depths. 'We had some good times. I'm grateful to you for that.'

'We had some fantastic times, darling! And I know now that it can never be the same with anyone else.'

'And you've had plenty of practice at finding out, have you?' She had turned and was looking at him with amused tolerance in her eyes.

'Oh, Eve, how can you be so cool and distant with me? With me, of all people?' He stood up and came towards her, catching hold of her hands and holding them tightly, so that she could not get free.

Eve resented being forced. Coldly she said, 'Mike, if I wanted to hold your hand, I would. I don't want to, and it's useless and caddish to make me.'

'Just say that—that—maybe you'll meet me again sometime. Next time you have some leave, maybe?' His voice was taut now, no longer genial and full of confidence in his powers of persuasion. 'Just make that promise, and I'll go away right now. Even though I'm starving, and don't know where I can get any lunch.'

Eve saw Anya moving about in the front room. She called her, and Mike reluctantly let go of her hands. 'Anya, Mr Grant will be staying for a little lunch, if that is all right with you.'

'Certainly, is all right.' Anya came to the door and Mike proceeded to practise his charm on her.

Eve excused herself, saying she had to see to the patients, and left Mike relaxing on the veranda with a glass of cold beer which the hospitable Anya had found in the fridge. It was very awkward to have him here. He was in the way, and Eve didn't want to make conversation with him. Yet it wasn't possible to send him

away without something to eat, and she only hoped
lunch would pass quickly.

Anya had placed plates of cold rice and vegetables on
the cloth, and had called Zaina to join them at the table,
when there was a shout from outside and Eve went to the
door, drawing back the curtain. A white-lipped youth
stood there, supporting a middle-aged Malay lady
who clung to his arm, bent over in obvious pain. 'My
mother, *lah*. Please help me. She got number one bad
pain.'

Zaina hurried to help Eve, who took the woman's
other arm and got her through to the ward. Mike stood
in the doorway. 'Can I help?' Eve laid the woman on a
bed, and stroked her furrowed forehead. 'Is it an acute
abdomen?' he questioned.

Eve was taking the woman's pulse. It seemed normal
and regular. The boy hovered from foot to foot beside
the bed. 'Pain is in chest, Sister. Is the heart, no?'

'Be quiet for a moment, please. I want your mother to
tell me exactly where the pain is.' She motioned Zaina to
pull a screen between them and the other patients.
'Now, point to where it hurts.'

Wincing, the woman indicated the centre of her chest,
and Eve touched with gentle fingers, pressing tentatively
under the ribs, until she knew from the woman's gasp
that she had found the pain. 'Well, I don't think it is your
heart, my dear. Let's just listen to it.' She took her
stethoscope, and carefully sounded the chest and back.
'Mmm. Nothing seems to be wrong there. Pass the
sphig, Zaina.' She wrapped the cuff round the thin arm,
and carefully took the blood pressure reading. 'That's
normal too.' She looked into the dark face, lined with
tension and pain. 'Does the pain come and go, or is it
there all the time?'

'Is there all the time, but sometimes worse.' It

appeared to be easing off, and the woman visibly relaxed against the white pillow.

'When did you last have something to eat? Is it worse after meals?'

She nodded, her drawn face clearing as the spasm left her. Eve patted her arm. 'Dr Craig will be here shortly. Rest for a while, and try to sleep. If it comes back, call me at once,' she said to the boy, who settled himself at his mother's bedside.

She went back into the front room. 'Well done,' Mike said. 'You want me to see her? What do you think it is?'

'Might be an ulcer.'

'Is the liver enlarged?'

'No. But it might be cholelithiasis.'

Mike frowned. 'What the hell do you do when you need a barium meal and a cholecystogram out here in the middle of nowhere?' And Eve found herself smiling at the city doctor's reaction—exactly like her own when she first came out to Dantang. 'Don't grin, girl. You need tests!'

Eve nodded. 'I know. And if necessary we will get her to Jahin. But the first rule out here is to wait and see. I have learned patience in the jungle, and also that expensive tests are not always needed. I'm going to wait for Andrew—Dr Craig. The patient is comfortable at the moment, and will come to no harm.' She was almost surprised at herself, at the calm confidence she had in Andrew and his unwritten rules. She would never have thought she would end up defending him so loyally.

'Well, thank you, lass.' A well-known dark brown voice said behind them. 'That is praise indeed.'

CHAPTER TEN

ANDREW CRAIG was framed in the doorway, holding aside the mosquito curtain with a lean brown hand. Eve could not prevent the leap of pleasure inside her at the sight of him, familiar, yet so impossibly unattainable. His face, once difficult for her to read, was open and relaxed as he looked around at them all, clearly glad to be back and also delighted to overhear Eve's comments.

Then he saw Mike Grant and his look vanished, replaced by a mask of cool professionalism. Eve caught the glance from herself to Mike and back again. Hastily she said, 'Hello, Andrew. This is Mike Grant. He's with the Harley Clinic in KL.'

Craig strode forward and grasped Mike's hand briefly. 'How do you do?' Then he turned to Anya and Zaina. His smile returned. 'How are you, ladies?'

'Okay, Doctor.'

'I hear you have a patient you want my advice about?'

Eve smiled. 'You heard right. I have a lady with GI symptoms. But it isn't clear whether her stomach or her gall bladder is causing the trouble. I thought you would be sure to have one of your diagnostic aids that would tell us.'

Craig was already going towards the ward, rolling up his shirt-sleeves ready to rinse his hands at the basin in the alcove. 'You're quite right, Eve.' But his tone towards her was no longer warm. He went into the ward and Eve first explained about the other two patients before steering him to the bed where the woman lay with her eyes closed, her son sitting sleepily at her side. They

143

quickly regained alertness when they realised Dr Craig was there.

He asked a few routine questions and then said suddenly, 'Do you drink buffalo milk, Mrs Tamar?'

She shook her head. 'I do not take milk.'

Craig said gently, 'Then I think I know what the trouble is. You will be all right here for a day or two, while I keep an eye on you. After that, I'll make an appointment for you to pop along to Jahin to see Mr Dalasingam. Okay?' He left both mother and son looking relieved and grateful.

Back in the front room, Anya had quickly made fresh coffee and they all sat around the table while Andrew explained. 'She doesn't take milk. That is probably because she doesn't like it—and that is probably because it gives her discomfort in the epigastrium. Logical?' He did not wait for an answer. 'If the poor lady had an ulcer, milk, being antacid, would ease the pain. As it does not do so, then the alternative would be that buffalo milk, containing fat, would cause trouble in the gall bladder.'

Mike Grant spoke. 'That's fair enough. But is it enough to judge?'

Andrew nodded. 'To begin with. At least I know which expensive test to order, instead of getting both done. But I'm not going to make a decision until I've seen her for a couple of days.' He turned to Anya. 'Make sure we have some milk in.' Anya nodded as she returned to the ward, with Zaina close behind her. 'I'll have a look at the other two later, unless you want me to see them now?' Andrew said.

Eve shook her head. 'No. It isn't urgent. Perhaps you'd like a rest, having driven so far.'

Andrew drained his coffee cup and stood up. 'A rest, yes—and I've a lot more gen for those tables you are doing for me. I'll sort it out a little for you.' He went to the door. 'Goodbye, Dr Grant. I assume you two want a little privacy.'

It was a barbed statement, said in a polite way, and Eve understood the heavy implication in his tone. Andrew thought there was something between them, and Eve thought it was a good idea to let him go on thinking that. Much as she hated to deceive him, she knew he would be more reluctant to be too much alone with her, which suited her while she was trying so hard to be loyal to Lisa.

Mike, however, was very anxious for there to be no misunderstanding, and before she could stop him he said in a similarly sarcastic tone, 'After meeting Dr Craig, I now understand why our engagement has been so decisively broken off.'

Her heart sank. Andrew had not yet left the room and he turned round at that remark, his piercing blue eyes scanning them both with hooded interest. 'You didn't tell me you had broken the engagement, Eve.'

Eve was suddenly angry. 'It wasn't your business. And I didn't break it, if you want to know. I came to KL as Mike's fiancée and found him besotted with his glamorous secretary, that's all.' She breathed deeply, knowing her face was flushed with irritation at them both. 'I came out here to work as a nurse, not to have my private life discussed and dissected.'

And most uncharacteristically, she found herself running from the room, pushing past Andrew, hot tears streaming down her cheeks. She flung herself on her bed, taking deep gasps as she tried to control her weeping. How could she have let him see how emotional she could be?

As her tears came under control, she heard voices downstairs. Male voices. Surely they could not be talking about her? She stole to the window. Andrew and

Mike were standing, in a not at all friendly manner, beside the monsoon drain. Through the window she heard Andrew say, 'I'll give you a lift to the garage, if you like. It's too hot to walk.'

Mike's voice was hard and angry. 'There's no need. I'll get off your patch quickly enough.' He crossed the bridge, and started off down the path. Then he turned. Andrew had not moved. Mike said, this time quietly, as though he regretted his rudeness, 'You're a lucky chap. Look after her.' And he set off rapidly, as though wanting no reply, soon disappearing round the bend towards Dantang.

'Look after her.' He had already assumed that Eve and Andrew were in the middle of an affair. And Andrew had not contradicted him. Eve crept back to bed and lay down, feeling totally drained, staring up at the little bright lizards on the ceiling, posing like jewels in the bright sunlight. How could she possibly keep her senses of loyalty to Lisa if Andrew knew she were heart-free and available for the odd physical comforts he might feel like sharing with her—while Lisa was away?

She turned over and lay face downwards, knowing that she was open now to terrible hurt. She dare not let things go any further with Andrew, because when he was reunited with Lisa, she knew she would not be able to carry on here. She would not be able to bear the sight of them together, as they had been when she first arrived—laughing at the same things, appreciating each other's company in that unique oriental way that so clearly was good for Andrew, something he needed more than he knew.

There was a gentle rap on the door and Andrew came in. Eve sat up, knowing her cheeks were flaming and her hair dishevelled, her lovely crisp uniform crumpled above her knees. 'I didn't tell you to come in,' she breathed, swallowing hard and pulling her skirt down quickly.

'I'm sorry.' His voice almost stopped her heart, with its liquid gentleness. 'I only came to apologise. It was appallingly bad manners, as you said. I had no right at all to speak of your private life. It won't happen again—I guess that Mike fellow riled me a little.'

He had left the way open. If she told him now that it was all right, she knew her resolve would crumple. There was nothing else to do. She must make it clear, right now, that Sister Carrol was not here to be played with while Lisa was away. She stood up, trying vainly to push her hair from her face, which was damp with sweat and tears. Making her voice as icy as she could, Eve said, 'You are so right. I hope from now on that nursing, and only nursing and my duties here, matter between us.'

There was a look on his face that touched her deeply. For a second his hand came out and helped her put back a stray lock of hair. Then he quickly drew away. He nodded, the blue eyes dark, and in a moment he was gone. She heard him go to his room and close the door gently. And she felt nothing but a beautiful glow where his hand had kissed her cheek with the delicacy of a butterfly's wing.

She slept for half an hour, knowing in her dreams that there were still tears on her face. Then she was suddenly alert, as she heard Zaina calling her name. She was up immediately. She brushed her hair back and splashed her face with water before running lightly downstairs. Zaina was on the veranda with a gentle-looking Malay woman holding a little girl of about two years old.

'Missy Eve, this is my cousin. She is visiting my mother and me from out at one village far away from here.' Zaina's face was tragic. 'And oh, Missy Eve, look at her child. Look at her eyes. My little flower, she is blind. Blind, so young.' Zaina's own eyes filled with tears as she gathered the pretty child in her arms, to show her to Eve more closely.

'What is her name?'

'Malika. She is such a sweet little girl. We all love her so much.'

Eve sat down and took Malika on her knee. She was light and dainty, with dark curls round a heart-shaped face and big dark eyes. But the eyes were dull, as though they had no moisture in them. Eve stroke back the curls and looked more closely.

There was another voice then, dark and controlled. 'Let's have a wee look, Eve.' She felt the warmth of his nearness and he bent over the child, took the tiny pulse. 'How old is she, Zaina?'

'Two and a half.'

'Mmm. Very thin, eh?'

'She always like this, Doctor. Fussy about her food. But always cheerful and full of energy.'

'Does she eat meat? Eggs?'

'No, she never liked them. Her parents are vegetarian.'

Andrew looked at Eve. 'What do you think, Eve?' His manner now was totally professional.

'Could it be vitamin A deficiency?'

He nodded, and he was smiling now. 'It could indeed. I'm glad to say, Zaina, that Malika can probably be cured completely. Have we any vitamin A?'

Zaina ran to look in the pharmacy, her feet light with relief. But she came back empty-handed. 'No, there is none.'

'Damn. How did that happen?'

Eve said, 'It must be my fault. Last time Balik came, I was sure I ordered it. But I didn't check when he brought the supplies in.'

'Then it is probably his fault!' Andrew was angry. 'Here is a kid with reversible blindness, and we don't have a simple remedy in stock. Well, I'm not leaving her like this. I'll drive into Jahin myself for some.'

Eve said quickly, 'No, no. Surely cod-liver oil will do? And I know Abbas's wife keeps that in her general store.'

'Good.' Andrew lost no time in explaining to Zaina and her cousin the importance of regular vitamin A and a balanced diet. And he gladly allowed Zaina the time off to go back with them to her home in Dantang.

'You are sure she will get her sight back?' Eve felt a natural tug at her heartstrings as they walked off with the little blind girl between them.

'Should be almost completely. Unless there is corneal scarring. But there was none visible to the naked eye, so I think we have caught it in time.' He stood up suddenly. 'I want to talk to Balik. If you ordered vitamin A and there is none in the pharmacy—'

'Oh no, don't take it out on him!'

Andrew swung round. 'You're in quite a rush to protect him.'

'You mustn't blame him. I was in charge. I should have checked.'

Andrew sat down. 'All right, you talk to him. But get those supplies—and fast.'

'I will,' she said, understanding his frustration. 'Just give me ten minutes to check the pharmacy, to make sure nothing else is missing.' But as she waited for Balik to answer the phone, Eve found herself siding with Andrew. Anything that was ordered ought to be here.

Balik was charmingly apologetic. 'I make the mistake, Eve. Tell your cross Dr Craig that it is not anything you did wrong. I take all the blame.'

'No one is cross, Balik. Just make a note that we want the supplies as soon as possible.'

'I will come at once, delightful lady. Expect me before dark.'

Eve couldn't help smiling to herself. 'You mean you want to join us for dinner?'

'I wouldn't dream of intruding.'

'Liar.'

'Oh well—if it is satay, no one does it better than Anya.'

'Balik, you are hopeless. Come, and welcome. Just don't forget what I've ordered this time.'

'Your vitamin A is written on my heart.'

Eve was still smiling at Balik's easy chatter. No wonder that he was popular throughout the region. He was quite a character. No one she knew was easier to like.

Andrew Craig made no reference to Balik when Eve returned to the veranda. The shadows were lengthening now, and the sun had lost its cruel heat. She sat down on the bamboo chair furthest away from him. 'So that is settled, then?' Andrew said.

'Yes. He will bring it later today.'

'Ah—then we may not be here.'

'Why not?' Eve felt resentment that Andrew should assume that he knew where she would be.

'The Sultan is expecting us for dinner. I'm sorry, I should have told you earlier. That Mike fellow drove it out of my mind.'

'I see.' Eve paused to let the idea sink in. They were going to dinner at the Palace. It was all arranged. Eve was flattered, but it had been a very emotional day and she was more than ready for an early night. 'I suppose it would be very rude to say no?'

'Extremely. I've already said yes.'

Eve did not reply. They sat together, looking out at

the jungle, which was now aflame with the scarlet of the sunset as it dropped behind the trees, flooding the sky with brilliance and glory. After a long time, Eve said conversationally, 'I expect you don't know that women like to have a day or two's notice, so that they can wash their hair, and have new dresses made—that sort of trivial little thing . . .'

'I do know.' His voice was abrupt. 'But you are the only woman I've met who can look good without preparation.'

'What do you mean?'

'I mean that whatever you wear, and whatever you are doing, Eve—you look right.' He did not look at her, but she sensed a lump in his throat. It was obviously a compliment he did not want to pay—but honesty prevailed.

She looked across at him for the first time. 'Do I detect a comment on my new uniform?'

He turned to face her, and their mutual smiles were direct and warm. 'Yes, you do. I must have seemed like a dinosaur to you, to make such a fuss about your sarong. I admit to you honestly—the uniform looks great. But I hope you'll wear the blue sarong tonight.' And their smiles did not fade when Andrew stood up and came to stand in front of her. Eve's poor heart could not object to his remarks. She felt like a lost lamb as she looked into his eyes, knowing that she would follow him to the moon if he so much as lifted a finger. He said quietly, 'Will you have one of my special brews now, or will you wait until we are both changed and ready to go?'

Something dragged her back to reality. 'I'll wait. But we both have a ward round to do first. One boy is ready to go home. He only had a septic wound in his foot. The other is worrying me. His pyrexia won't seem to settle. And there are no other symptoms. I know Q fever is not

common in Malaysia, but none of the symptoms points
to anything else. And according to his history, he works
as a buffalo herdsman.'

Andrew Craig looked down at her, outlined against
the sky. 'My dear lassie!'

'What exactly does that mean? Am I being very
stupid?'

He shook his head, smiling. 'Come on, let's have a
look at him.' And as she stood up, he went on, 'I told you
I recognised I had a treasure. Tell me, Eve—where did
you read up about Q fever?'

'I didn't.' She had to be honest. 'A friend told me
about it before I left Britain. I must say I wouldn't have
thought of it, except that his heart rhythm is a bit
irregular—and of course, his job.'

Andrew nodded. 'Almost all cases are in people who
work with animals. Well, let's have a look, shall we?'

Eve felt insecure. Perhaps she had made a mistake
here and missed some very obvious symptom. She ought
not to have mentioned her suspicion; she should have
waited until Andrew had examined the lad. So she
watched with bated breath as Andrew took a careful
history and then proceeded to a thorough and slow
physical examination. He took especially long over
listening to the boy's heart, and Eve knew he was
listening for any sign at all that the heart valves were
damaged. When she had listened herself, she knew that
her own experience was not sufficient to decide. If there
was damage, it was very slight at the moment.

She watched as Andrew straightened up and took the
stethoscope from his ears. He felt the boy's head again
and indicated that he could lie back and relax. Then
Andrew turned round from where he was sitting on the
bed. He looked up into Eve's face. 'Have we any
Lincomycin?'

'Yes.' She breathed out. She had been right. His diagnosis agreed with hers. 'I got it out. It's in the office.'

It was seven o'clock. They were both coming out of their rooms at the same time. Andrew was wearing dark trousers and a white shirt with a black bow tie. Eve wore Lisa's pastel blue sarong and her newly-washed hair curled naturally on her shoulders. As Andrew caught up with her at the top of the stairs he smiled, and held out his arm. She could not but take his elbow, although she made sure it was only a light and non-committal hold. He bent his head towards hers. 'Anya told me about the stricter routine in the ward.'

Eve waited with a feeling of foreboding. He was going to tell her it was not necessary.

'I want to thank you. You've done a superb job. Without this extra diligence, young Misra could easily have been sent home with a course of aspirin.'

Eve glowed. She smiled up at Andrew without reserve. And she felt safe. He was praising her nursing, not her appearance. 'Thanks. It means a lot. You are a hard man to please, but I knew if I got the chance, I could do this job properly.'

They reached the bottom of the stairs and Andrew let go her arm so that he could go to his cupboard and play with his array of bottles. With his back to her he said, 'There's never been a woman in my life whom I admire as much as I do you.'

She said nothing. But her mind swam with pictures of the girl he had adored when he was a young man, the surgeon with a career-oriented life. And with her was the image of dainty Lisa, with her porcelain face and limpid eyes following Andrew with total devotion and admiration. The simple sentence he had just pronounced set her above both of these ideal images. Eve felt ashamed. She ought not to feel so glad to have that statement from him. It meant so much that she felt he probably did not mean.

She left him and went through the curtain to the veranda without answering him. The night was clear, but there were a few clouds that threatened the bright new moon. Eve watched them, waiting for the happiness in her heart to die down. Andrew had only praised her for good diagnosis. It didn't mean more than that. Yet she couldn't stop herself from reading into that one sentence all she had dreamed of hearing from him. And her guilt swept over her as she thought of Lisa, already by now preparing to return to Dantang, probably longing to see the tall Scotsman with his black brows and gruff manner, whom she had already made clear she admired with all her heart.

There was a murmuring noise from the jungle path. It coughed and spluttered. Then it growled, and Eve recognised the temperamental engine of Balik's little Japanese wreck, which he drove so dashingly about the countryside.

And as Balik zoomed up to the car park and jumped out of the car, an idea came to Eve. Here was a diversion—a man she could pretend to be interested in. That would save her conscience and also show Andrew that she was still not available, even after his admission of admiration—which, she had to admit, had sounded very grudging, the more she thought about it.

She ran across the bridge to meet Balik. She had forgotten that she was dressed up, with her silver earrings and her best French perfume. Balik, however, was not the man to ignore such things.

'Eve, *maharani!* What a beautiful princess you look tonight!' He slammed the car door, and came towards her with both hands outstretched. 'Am I permitted a kiss?'

Eve looked back. Andrew was just coming out, his hands holding two glasses. She turned to Balik. 'Just this once,' she said, and put her hands on his shoulders while he kissed her lightly on both cheeks.

There. No doubt about that. Andrew couldn't have missed it. Eve waited while Balik took a couple of cartons of supplies from the boot of the car and they walked back to the veranda together. 'Good evening, Dr Craig.' Balik was polite, knowing that the dour Craig did not usually welcome his company. 'I apologise for the mistake. I come all the way from Kuanang to make up for this.'

'Thanks. I hope it doesn't happen again.' Craig's face was stony. He indicated the drinks. 'Here, have mine. I'll go and get another.' And he left them alone on the veranda. Eve felt a heel, yet it had been the only thing to do. What she must do now is make sure Balik did not get the wrong idea as well.

'I'm afraid we won't be here for dinner, Balik. We're going out.'

The young pharmacist nodded, apparently not unduly bothered. He picked up the cocktail and toasted Eve with a little bow. 'That is okay. I ought not to be too late. I am hoping Lisa will ring from Singapore to tell me which plane she is getting back. I have offered to meet her in KL.'

'That is awfully kind,' Eve smiled.

'That is me, Eve. The soul of kindness, you know.' He grinned and finished the drink. 'And I am very sorry about the drugs. I will make sure it does not happen again, *lah*.'

She nodded. 'Not to worry. Thanks again, Balik. *Terimasakih. Selamat tinggal, kawan.*'

He tilted his head to one side, smiling at her pronunciation. 'Yes, *maharani*. Goodbye, my friend. I will see you in a day or two, when I bring your lovely Lisa back to you.'

'That's fine, Balik. *Baiklah*. I will send the money at the end of the month as usual.'

'Fine, fine.' He lifted a hand in salutation and jumped down the two steps from the veranda. In a moment, the car door slammed again and he was urging the plucky little vehicle down the dirt road. The last of the sunset sent dark shadows chasing him, as the chugging of the engine faded into the peace of the night.

Eve sat down alone and sipped her drink. Andrew was clearly avoiding her now, and although it was what she had planned, she felt sad at the same time. Just as she had pretended that Mike mattered to her, now she was being equally deceitful with Balik. The only consolation was that it was in a very good cause. Lisa would be back in a couple of days, and Eve felt that she had survived with her heart intact. The attractive Scotsman would soon have other charms to turn his devastating blue eyes on.

'So you had no problems with the bandits, Eve?' He had returned, obviously determined not to talk about her private affairs, as he had promised.

'Not a sign, thank goodness.' But she had had her problems with the Bomoh, and soon poured out the tale of Haria, of finding her clothes, and the way the villagers had ganged up against her that day in the village. 'I wonder if they will ever trust me as they do you,' she said wistfully.

Andrew was silent for a moment. He picked up his glass and twisted it around in his elegant fingers. 'Yes, I can see something will have to be done about the Bomoh. He is insanely jealous of you, that's plain enough.' He drained the Martini. 'Come on. Let's set off. I'll work out something soon. If you are going to work here in any sort of peace, I shall have to sort that fellow out.'

'Thank you. I'm not afraid, exactly, but I want the people to look on me as a friend.'

They walked down to the Rover in the moonlight. He opened the door for her and let himself into the driving seat, and they set off down the now familiar stretch of road. He didn't speak as they drove, and a sidelong glance showed Eve that his jaw was set, his lips in a tight line, showing that he was a lot less relaxed than his easy conversation had indicated. She felt a surge of compassion towards him. In an effort to help, she said, 'Lisa will be back in a day or two.'

His expression did not change. 'Good.'

She looked again, puzzled at the lack of response. 'You did hear what I said?'

'Mmm? Yes. Lisa is coming back.'

'She is a wonderful person. So full of serenity and grace. I've missed her.'

'You have?' He turned to look at her briefly. 'It didn't show.' Eve was not sure how to take this remark. Either he did not care too much whether Lisa was here or elsewhere, or he was disguising his feelings very well. They had turned off now, to the Palace road, and were going along in the full glare of the headlamps. The sliver of moon had disappeared behind the clouds, which had now become more threatening. Andrew said, 'If you were wanting to know what I think about Lisa, I'll tell you. She is a dedicated and loyal friend.'

CHAPTER ELEVEN

'BUT what—?'

'Here we are.' Andrew braked gently in front of the Palace wall and switched off the engine. He looked across at her, his face still serious. 'You asked me to respect your privacy, Eve. Do you mind if I make the same request?' His voice was very low.

'I'm sorry.' Now she felt dreadful, as though she had been caught looking through his private papers. 'I really didn't intend to be so blatant. I only wanted to—well,—to cheer you up a little.'

'You did? You felt sorry for me? Well, that's sweet. Maybe you are learning some oriental ways at last.' But she could not read in his tone whether he was sincere, or making fun of her. She got out of the car without any further comment. The immaculate footmen were already waiting to bow them into the hall and take the Rover away to the covered car park. All she knew at that moment was that they were going to a dinner party, when she wanted more than anything to sit somewhere quiet and talk to no one else but Andrew Craig. She felt at that moment that she was almost on the point of getting through to the real man behind the strong, silent mask.

The tall Indian butler was waiting at the door. With a low bow, he welcomed them both. 'Dr Craig, His Highness awaits you in the library. Miss Carrol, would you come this way? Her Highness is in her apartments with Madame Dalasingam.'

Eve followed him along the corridor, the deep blue

158

and turquoise tiles contrasting with the white walls and
the huge arrangements of red and white flowers. In spite
of her initial reluctance to come out to dinner, there was
no doubt that being at the Palace was an exciting experience. And she was pleased to see the Sultana looking so
well. The little lady came towards her with outstretched
hands.

'How nice to see you. I am so very grateful to you for
the way you helped us, and allowed Andrew to come
with me to hospital. It made so much difference, I assure
you.'

'It is all part of the job, ma'am.'

Her Highness held up a transparent hand. At least, so
it looked, it was so white and delicate. 'I want you to call
me by my name. And I also have a small gift for you. Do
come into my bedroom.' She beckoned and Eve followed the graceful figure, dressed tonight in emerald
green silk, with matching gems in her ears and glittering
in her hair. Standing near the white and gold dressing-
table stood Mina Dalasingam.

'Hello, Eve. I am glad to see you again.' The tall
Indian woman was in dark red, and she came forward,
her bangles jingling on her slim arms, to kiss Eve warmly
on the cheek. 'Zamina was just showing me what she has
had made for you. Come and look.'

On the white brocade bed-cover lay a sarong kebaya
in turquoise Thai silk, with deep borders of gold thread.
'You paid us the compliment of wearing our national
costume, so I have made one for you. Do try it, Eve. I
hope you like the colour.'

'It is magnificent.' Eve was overwhelmed. She
changed into the skirt first, wrapping the smooth silk
around her body with practised ease by now, folding the
fullness of the sarong to the front and securing it in the
waistband. Then she picked up the blouse, delicate and

exotic, with tiny sleeves and a rounded neckline edged
with gold. 'I have never owned anything half so beautiful!' She paraded in front of the tall mirror, surprised
that the elegant creature she saw there was indeed Eve
Carrol.

'Now we will go and have some champagne.' Zamina
was well pleased with the reaction to her gift. 'After all, I
wanted to show my gratitude in a way that would really
please you.' The three women walked along the corridor
towards the conservatory, where the men were already
standing between the potted palms and the orchids,
sipping champagne and talking with the ease of old
friends. The sky outside was overcast, but the gardens
were visible, lit by concealed lighting, that showed off
the fountains and a small lake covered with water lilies,
surrounded by tall cypresses and palms. Eve began to
feel that it was all part of a dream, so different was it
from her life at Dantang so far.

The Sultan and the surgeon greeted her warmly. And
as the servant brought them a silver tray with tall glasses
of cool champagne, it was Andrew who took a glass and
handed it to her, taken aback as he was by her regal
appearance. 'This isn't the woman who came with me,'
he whispered.

'It is a present from the Sultana.'

'Does it come complete with its own glass slippers?'

Eve laughed. 'I do hope it doesn't turn to rags at
midnight!'

'Come, come, Andrew. No monopolising Eve in a
corner.' The Sultan was at his sunny best, clearly pleased
to have his wife well and to have an evening with his
friends where he could relax completely. 'Though, I
must say, she is looking exceptionally lovely tonight.'

'Dantang suits you, that is clear.' Mr Dalasingam
added his praise. 'You are quite at home there now?'

'I think so. The routine and I have come to terms,' she smiled. 'Only the Bomoh makes his feelings known.'

'The Bomoh? That crazy fellow with the monkey skulls? I didn't think he was around any more.' The Sultan had heard many stories over the years, but he was concerned when Andrew told him what had been taking place. 'I will see what I can do. He may be harmless, but he is certainly a nuisance.'

Eve was anxious to change the subject. She didn't want to talk about herself, but to hear about the glamorous life that was commonplace to the Sultan and his friends. It was another world, where wishes became reality just as readily as though they owned a lamp with a genie in it. She listened, wide-eyed, as the other talked and laughed about trips to Bali, to Monaco, California and Gleneagles.

The dinner table shone with burnished Thai silver, white damask, glittering crystal and tumbling masses of brown and white spider orchids. Eve was glad she was placed opposite Andrew, so that she could secretly study the lean, handsome face, a face she thought she would never tire of looking at. He was attentive to his hostess, yet she could tell that his conversation was sometimes forced, that he would have preferred, like herself, to observe, rather than to take part in the cheerful gathering.

The food was brought on silver platters, fragrant and delectable. There was salad, elegantly served. The vegetables were tender and fresh, almost as many as Eve had ever heard of, and a few that she had never seen before. There were tiny fishes in a tangy sauce. There were small spiced pieces of duck, chicken and guinea fowl. There were kebabs of mutton, tinged with a delightful flavour and served with mushrooms and green peppers. The rice was scented, delicately coloured with saffron and sprinkled with cashew nuts.

Somehow, Eve was drawn into the conversation again and the story of her lost suitcase was recounted. They agreed that it had probably been taken by local bandits who, disgusted at the contents, gave them to the old woman, Haria, to sell. The Sultan said, 'By all accounts, losing that uniform put your chief in quite a bad mood.' He was grinning at Andrew, who managed a crooked smile with a certain air of reluctance.

Eve nodded. 'He *was* a bit disapproving.'

'Disapproving? That isn't what I heard. I heard you looked so stunning that he couldn't keep his mind on his work.' His Highness leaned over and said, 'And I can quite believe it, too.'

There was a general outburst of laughter, and then the conversation turned to other matters. But as Eve lifted her eyes from her plate, she saw that Andrew Craig was actually blushing. He lifted his wine glass to cover his confusion and Eve felt angry with them for being so insensitive. She knew the kindly Sultan meant no harm. But she began to long for the evening to be over.

They went out to the garden again for their coffee. The sky was definitely black, with not a star in sight, though the atmosphere was hot and close. Strong, fragrant coffee was served in fine china cups. Eve found herself next to the Sultana, who whispered, 'I remember you telling me that you thought you had nothing in common with Andrew.'

Eve reddened. 'Yes, I know. I didn't know him so well then.'

'I think you get along very well. You are good for him, I think. He speaks of you so very warmly.'

Eve felt a great sadness at the gentle words. If only the Sultana knew what she was saying. Eve said softly, 'We get on well, yes. But I believe there is someone else who is much better for him than I.'

'Surely not? We are his friends. He would have told us, I'm sure.'

Eve stifled a sigh. 'Perhaps he doesn't know himself yet.'

'My dear,' the Sultana's big, almond eyes were full of concern, 'I didn't think you cared so very much.'

'I don't, truly. No, I don't. I just—well, understand him, I think. You can't help that, you know, when you work with someone.' Eve knew the words were tumbling out too fast. She ought not to have had so much champagne. She stood up and turned towards the garden—only to find that she was standing close by the white pillar where Andrew had kissed her the first time.

'My dear Eve, I didn't mean to upset you.' The Sultana leaned towards her and touched her cheek with her soft little fingers. 'I won't say another word. Come and have more coffee.'

'Yes, thank you.'

'And will you come and visit me sometimes? Perhaps the afternoons, when you are quiet? Come and take tea with me.'

'I would love to.'

'Good. Now I know I haven't offended you.'

'You couldn't do that.' Eve found herself smiling. 'You seem to be so good at being a hostess. I have never had such a wonderful evening in my life.'

'I am happy.' And Eve began to thank her again for the sarong, but she shook her head. 'I have arranged for the one you were wearing to be put in the car.'

Andrew came over to join them, adding his thanks to the gentle Zamina. 'But you will forgive us if we go now? I know you like to play a little bridge after dinner, and—'

'And you are no card player. Or so you pretend, every

time I ask you,' she scolded him prettily. 'I shall make
Eve a player too, then we can both bully you to join in.'
And Eve thought wistfully that the Sultana was making
plans for them both that could not possibly come true.

They did not speak for the first few miles of the jungle
road. Then Eve ventured, 'I am invited for tea sometime
soon.'

Andrew said rather brusquely, 'I hope you will go.
She likes you and she is very lonely, for all the social
whirl that Edward talks about. Her illness doesn't allow
for a full social life. Most of the people she meets are
very casual acquaintances, rather than real friends.'

'I'd love to go.'

'I hope you didn't mind being dragged away? I can't
stand bridge.'

'Neither can I.' The difference between them was that
Eve would have played if asked, purely out of polite-
ness. Andrew was too honest. She looked at the craggy
profile, admiring his integrity, admiring his taciturn
gruffness more at this moment than any polished but
empty compliment.

They said no more. It was after twelve when they drew
up under the trees and Andrew tugged at the handbrake
and turned off the engine. Then he sat motionless, and
Eve waited, not wanting to disturb his thoughts. The
cicadas in the grass all around them filled the glade with
their chirping chorus.

'I won't come in.'

'Why?'

'I wouldn't want to compromise you.'

'That's rubbish. You never bothered before.'

He turned to her then, and pushed his fingers wearily
through his dark hair. Eve felt a sudden impulse to
stroke it back and soothe the worried look from his
forehead. Then she realised it must be because Lisa was

coming back. He was remembering where his loyalty lay. He didn't want to compromise her—or himself. And they both knew that the chemistry between them was very volatile. 'I'm sorry. I shouldn't have spoken to you like that.'

'You can speak to me any way you want, lass.' His voice was low and tired. Then he made an effort to smile. 'And if you looked like Cinderella at the party,' he touched one of her dangling filigree earrings, 'you look even lovelier now.'

Eve felt for the door handle and opened the door. 'That,' she said firmly, 'is because it is pitch black, and you can't see me at all.'

She had hoped that a light-hearted tone would lift his mood a little, but his words cut into her heart by their very gentleness. 'I can see you, Eve. I'll always see you.'

She got out of the car, her throat suddenly constricted by tears. She dare not say good night. She walked away from him, knowing very well that half of herself was still with him, and always would be. She stumbled a little on the grassy tussocks. The little electric bulb on the veranda was not much use until she had crossed the monsoon drain. The air was sticky and oppressive. There would surely be a storm before dawn.

She heard the ignition whirr. The engine turned, but Andrew made no attempt to press the accelerator. Eve went on, up the steps, and pulled the mosquito curtain to one side. The Rover was still purring. She let the curtain drop and reached out to put on the small table lamp.

Then she saw him! A tall, bony, dark-skinned figure, his lips open in an attempt at a smile, showing gaps between bad teeth. The Bomoh! Eve screamed as his expression came alive at the sight of her. He took a step towards her. She backed away. 'No! Oh, no!'

Suddenly Andrew was by her side. His arms came

round her and she turned, burying her head in his chest, holding him tight. 'What is it? It's all right, my lass, I'm here.' And she pressed herself against him, her heart thumping against her ribs, unwilling to look at the scarecrow who stood in the room with them.

Then she looked up into Andrew's face. He stroked her hair as, with more confidence, she turned again to face the Bomoh. But the gangling figure was not the insane creature with a knife in his hand. He was looking more afraid that they were. He stood, sheepish and apprehensive, his bony wrists and fingers sticking out from a ragged shirt that was a size or two too small for him. It was those fingers that Eve recognised. She had last seen them clutching at the thin coverlet as they carried him, light as a baby, to the waiting ambulance.

She let go of Andrew, feeling ashamed of herself. 'Jacko? It is Jacko, isn't it?' He grinned then, and Eve moved out of the protective circle of Andrew's arms and advanced towards the visitor. 'I am sorry. I shouldn't have screamed. But I wasn't exactly expecting you, Jacko.'

He spoke, in a husky but firm voice. 'I come back, Missy Carrol. I come back to say thank you. You not here, and I fall asleep on the floor until I hear the car. I not wish for to make you frighten, Missy Carrol. Not ever, *lah*.'

Andrew stepped forward and reached for the man's thin hand, shaking it warmly. 'It is good to see you, Jacko. You know you owe your life to Sister Carrol? That I had nothing to do with it?' But the man's wide smile of thanks was including them both, none the less. 'You have eaten?'

'Yes, Tuan Doctor. Anya, she give me plenty rice, plenty of dhal. She say there is work in the garden, if you say okay, *lah*? I want for to work for nothing, Tuan.'

Eve felt tears pricking her eyelids. She looked at Andrew, hoping he would not send the poor fellow away. He said briskly, 'Come and see me in the morning, Jacko. We'll arrange something.' The grateful Malay clasped his thin hands together and bowed to them both. Andrew walked with him to the path, before coming in again and closing the door. He smiled ruefully at Eve. 'You were right, Eve. I never thought he had a chance in hell.'

'Neither did I. I just thought he ought to be given the chance.'

'That is what I should have thought.' He looked down at her, his eyes honest. 'You have certainly taught me a thing or two in the last few weeks, Sister Carrol.'

She nodded, not really trusting herself to speak. She knew he was going to stay. He had closed the door behind him. And because she felt strangely childlike and vulnerable, after that shock when she thought the Bomoh was here, and she knew there was nothing she wanted more than to be embraced, comforted and cherished, she turned and went upstairs to bed without saying anything else, in case it was the wrong thing.

She listened to him as he left his shoes at the door and came upstairs to his own room, passing her door. His step was quiet, yet she felt as though she knew exactly where he was by some strange new sense she had developed since meeting him. She imagined him lying as she was, under the thin sheet, watching the fan swing round and round and listening to the occasional swift scutter of the lizards as they changed position.

The rain began with first light, slipping and slopping as though it was being thrown from some huge bucket. Great chunks of water thudded against the sides and roof of the hospital, as though trying to cave it in. There was little chance of a clinic today. Even Jacko would not venture from the village with the path so suddenly muddy and treacherous again. Zaina, also, would not be able to get here. And little Danny, whose foot was much better, would not be able to get home, unless he were to be taken in the car.

'So, Anya, there are only the three of us for today.' Andrew smiled at the little woman as she served up a breakfast of bacon and eggs on the usual spotless white cloth.

'Yes, Doctor. If you get bored, I'll find you something to do in the kitchen, yes?'

He and Eve both laughed. They had already decided that it was very good weather for writing up some of the research he had done during his few days away. Eve was to tabulate the results, while he got on with the actual writing of the paper. 'You see, Eve—I was right about the plantation being a father-figure to Dantang. The health of the villagers is really better than at the other three places I visit. Just look at the amount of diseases they have that are caused by faulty nutrition.'

Eve went through the lists he had drawn up, fascinated by the extremes of health education within a fairly small area. 'You said the government wants a copy of this?'

'Yes. The health minister is a great chap. He'll do his best to put this right. But it will take time, of course. Dantang has had its plantation and hospital for a hundred years.'

'I hope it'll take a bit less than that,' she laughed.

They pored over the charts and lists, working so easily and well together that it would have been impossible to tell that the same two people had been afraid to touch each other last night in case the ensuing explosion damaged more than themselves. Yet Eve did not see, when her fair head was bent over the bulky files, how Andrew stopped his work and gazed on that head, admiring the highlights in her hair and the way the tendrils curled on the tanned little neck.

Anya was doing the temperatures. They had all been to see Misra, who was still fevered, but a lot more comfortable since being put on the antibiotic. He felt well enough to play draughts with young Danny, who was hopping about, using a crutch to keep the weight off his poisoned foot. 'Have you any cards? I know a lot of magic tricks,' he was boasting. When Anya found him a pack, he soon had her and Misra highly amused, not only by his skill, but by his attempts at a slick American accent.

The patients slept after lunch. Eve and Andrew worked on for a little while, but soon Eve yawned, and they decided to leave it for a while. There was nothing outside but the endless drone of raindrops falling in their millions all around them.

'You go and rest. We'll work better if we are fresh,' Andrew suggested. She knew he was watching her as she left the room. She knew that he too wanted a rest, but was deliberately staying downstairs to avoid any chance encounters in the corridor.

She was all the more surprised, then, to be woken by him, holding a cup of tea. 'Had enough sleep?'

She sat up. 'Yes, thank you. But what's with the tea? Is there work to do?'

He shook his head. 'No work. But your boyfriend has turned up. I thought you'd like to know. Must be pretty fond of you to plough through this weather, I'd say.'

She frowned. His face was a mask of oriental impassiveness. 'I haven't got a boyfriend. You don't mean Mike Grant, do you? He wouldn't be such an idiot.'

Andrew said calmly, 'No, not Mike. I'll be working in my room if you want me.'

'No, wait. You know there's no one I want to talk to alone.' But he had closed the door gently behind him with an air of finality. Eve drank the tea, washed her face and went downstairs, curious and a little hurt by Andrew's attitude.

'Mr Balik, Kuanang's answer to Boots!' She smiled at him, as he sat finishing his cup of tea. 'What brings you here?'

'It's Lisa. She hasn't rung me. And when I tried to get her, her sister said she had left.'

'She has left Singapore? So she is on the way at the moment?'

'Yes. Have you any idea what time to expect her?'

'No, none. I didn't think she would set off without telling anyone.'

Balik nodded. 'That is what is bothering me. I might have been in the back of the shop and not heard the phone. You see, the weather is only bad around here. She may not know that we are in danger of being cut off altogether, *lah*.'

The telephone rang at that moment and they both dashed into the corridor. 'Hello?'

'Eve, dear, it's Lisa. I'm in a phone box at the airport.'

'Where? What airport? Not Kuala Lumpur already?'

'Yes. The flight got in early. I'll just take a cab, and I'll be with you before midnight, I hope. I won't—'

'Lisa, for goodness' sake, listen to me. You can't just set off like that. Look, Balik is here. He's ready to—'

'You mustn't dream of wasting all that time. I've got the cab waiting. See you soon.'

'Lisa, no!' Eve shook the receiver. 'She's hung up.' She faced Balik, and they both shrugged their shoulders. 'What do we do now?'

'Well, I suppose she will get half-way, and then the cab driver will decide that he's not going to risk his cab as soon as they hit the bad weather. So when he decides that, they'll stop—and Lisa will have to stay in a hotel for the night. My guess is that she'll phone us when that happens, and then—presto—I'll go along and fetch her from there.'

Eve led the way back to the room. 'You make it sound simple.'

'Well, it is, *lah*. Don't look so worried, Princess. Lisa is a very sensible lady. She knows how to take care of herself.'

'Well, yes. I can't argue with that.'

'In fact, it is better. I will have less mileage to do—and she will have the delightful company of the best-looking chemist in Selangor.'

Eve allowed herself a smile. 'She might even like that.'

'So, cheer up, and join me in a song.'

'In a what?' Eve was standing at the window, staring out at the endless streaming rain, like some moving mirror in front of the dark trees.

There was a sudden strumming behind her. She turned and smiled again as she saw the irrepressible Balik holding up a battered guitar. 'Just another of my many talents. Never travel without it, especially when it looks like rain. I've been marooned in many a lonely hospital, with nothing to entertain those lonely little nurses but that box in the corner that makes funny faces at you and talks American.'

'We are going to get a TV. Anya had one but it broke down, and no one knew how to repair it.'

Balik strummed. Then he launched into 'A Hard Day's Night'. After a couple of lines, he stopped. 'Go and get Anya—and the good doctor. Tell them their troubles are over. No need to be bored when Balik's around.'

Eve shook her head, amused in spite of herself. 'You might be more good in the ward. Those two lads would enjoy a live show, I'm sure.'

Balik strummed again. 'You got it, Sister.' He played a quick arpeggio, and started gaily, 'We're off to see the Wizard, the wonderful Wizard of Oz.' She followed him to the ward. Anya and the patients were delighted at the prospect of some singing and Eve left them calling out requests and went back to the front room.

There was no one there. She sat down in an armchair. She could hear the music through the open door and along the corridor. Balik played quite well, and his voice was good. But she found that her thoughts were very unsettled at the thought that Lisa was so near home. She knew she was dreading the way Andrew's face would brighten at her gentle presence, the way he would seize her hands, and look into those warm brown eyes with their incredible lashes . . . And she heard Balik change key, and start,

'Yesterday, love was such an easy game to play
Now I need a place to hide away
Oh I believe
In yesterday . . .'

The simple words touched her already overwrought feelings. She put her head in her hands, feeling tears creeping between her fingers. He could have played anything else but that.

She became lost in her own thoughts, so she jumped with surprise when there was a gentle touch on her shoulder. 'Balik. But the music . . .'

'That boy, Misra. He can play. I left them to see where you had gone.'

'I was listening, Balik, honestly. But I wanted a little time to myself. I have a bit of thinking to do.'

The smooth, sincere face was looking at her more shrewdly than she wanted. 'You have been crying.'

'It is your fantastic playing,' she tried to joke.

'Eve—I am a clown sometimes. But I know when somebody is sad. Is there anything I can do? You like to talk?'

'I guess I'd love to talk. But it would do no good at all. In fact, I'd much rather listen to your music. It's soothing and pretty, and it shuts out the sound of the rain on the roof.'

He went away without a word and came back with the guitar. He sat on the floor at her feet and began to play very softly, his voice tender. She looked down into his face as he sang, her feelings at the same time touched and soothed.

She was not to know the picture they made in the fading light—the blonde English girl in her pale sarong, her head tilted to one side, her blue eyes dreamy, and the dashing young Malay, with his mop of black curls and the muscles in his naked arms rippling as he sang his gentle words up to her.

There was a silence as the song came to an end. It was shattered by a sharp remark from the doorway. 'You do know the phone is dead?' Andrew stood there, aloof and cold.

'I didn't realise it was dead. That must be why Lisa's call was cut off so abruptly. We didn't have a chance to tell her how bad the roads are around here.' Eve felt that Andrew's anger was because Balik was a rival for Lisa, and she sympathised with him in her heart. There was now no thought of calling this man bad-tempered, or

Attila the Hun. How could she ever, now that she knew him as well as she did?

'She won't be so reckless as to try to make the journey in this.' Andrew, too, appeared to have confidence in Lisa's good sense. 'She knows how bad it can be.'

'Andrew,' Eve turned to him, appealing, 'do come and sit here. Listen to the guitar. Balik plays well.'

'I can hear that.' Andrew made no move to join them. 'But you must excuse me. I have some work to catch up on.'

CHAPTER TWELVE

IT WAS dark, and still raining. Eve did the final ward round alone, feeling that Andrew was in no mood to be disturbed. Her patients were pleasantly tired after the stimulating change of Balik's cheery presence. She left them in Anya's charge and went back to the front room.

The table was laid for three. Balik was sitting quietly, listening to the rain. He looked up and said quietly, 'You'd better get Dr Craig or he won't get any dinner.'

She nodded. 'Why are you sitting in the dark?'

'I don't need light to think.'

She looked down on the tousled head. 'So you think too, do you?' He looked up at her and nodded gravely. Eve patted the dark head, as she would a pet dog, and passed him to put on the lamps.

Anya came in with a tray of steaming dishes. Eve went upstairs in the dark, seeing the gathering dusk outside the window, desolate, green-grey jungle through a curtain of water.

Andrew was sitting in the dark at his desk, as still as a dead man. 'Are you all right? Dinner is on the table.'

He turned to look at her. 'Yes, I'm all right.' His tone was dead too. She looked into his face in the gloom, moved by the attitude of his usually lithe body, now leaning, reflecting the desolation outside. Was he really so sad at the presence of young Balik? Couldn't he see how much Lisa cared for him? Balik was a fine man, but in Eve's opinion, not even in Craig's league. How would he look so depressed when he was definitely the better man?

The fan turned in the ceiling with a slight, regular creak. Andrew said in a low voice, 'That's all right, lass. I'll be along. Go on, now.' But she did not go. For some reason her feet wouldn't move, and the tears that Balik's song had inspired now began to gather again in her eyes and slip down her cheeks. She was glad it was too dark for Andrew to see them.

There was a sharp bird call, as some soaking creature in the jungle voiced a harsh protest at the weather. Eve said, for the sake of breaking the silence, 'I've always liked it when you call me lass.'

He turned round in his chair and caught her round the waist, hugging her against him, his face against her breast. She held him, one hand stroking his hair, as she had wanted to do so many times, comforting him and being comforted. This was probably the last time she would feel him in her arms. And the thought hurt her so much that one of her tears fell on to his face and he stirred, feeling with one hand her wet cheeks. 'Eve?' He stood up, suddenly stimulated. 'Eve, what is it?'

Outside there was a sudden loud commotion, voices calling and lights flashing. Someone was calling—'Doctor! Doctor!' They both turned to the window, where they could see two villagers struggling up the road towards the hospital. 'Trouble. Come on,' Andrew said. They ran downstairs and out on to the veranda, where Anya and Balik were already helping the two men in.

'Sister Carrol, Tuan Doctor—an accident near the village. A car come off road.'

The other man chipped in. 'Did not come off road. Road collapse in rain.'

'Who is hurt?' Andrew was already getting the emergency pack from a cupboard, and checking the drugs in the lid.

'We do not know. We see no one. Car turn over, right

over. Water all around.' His honest face was twisted with darkness. 'Oh Tuan, we try to telephone you, but no line up. You come quickly?'

'Of course. Anya, have we any rope?'

'Yes, yes.' The good woman scurried off and came back with a clothes line.

Balik said quickly, 'I'll come. How many torches have you? I have a couple in my car.'

Eve slung the emergency bag on to Andrew's back. 'Shall I come too?' The two men were ready, opening the door and pulling on their shoes, as the villagers prepared to lead the way. Balik ran across the full monsoon drain towards his Toyota and brought the torches.

Andrew looked back at Eve. 'No, just be ready. If there is anyone alive, these chaps can give us a hand with the stretchers.'

They started off down the road, now a quagmire, slipping and sliding, holding on to the trees to steady themselves as they went. She heard Balik say in Malay, 'You know whose car it was?'

The reply came, like a stab of lightning. 'Nobody from Dantang. It was a cab from Kuala Lumpur.'

A cab, upside down in a sea of mud and water. Eve froze. 'Oh, Anya!' The women clutched at each other in mutual despair and apprehension. 'There is nothing we can do, Anya. We just have to wait. It will take at least half an hour to get down there in these conditions.'

Anya said stolidly, 'I put the food to keep warm, *lah*. They will need to eat when they get back.'

Anything to keep busy. Eve's thoughts kept tumbling over themselves. Oh, Lisa, dear little Lisa, don't be hurt. Hold on, Lisa, they are coming to get you. She saw in her mind's eye the four men fighting their way to the village, their muscles straining, their breathing laboured

and their own hearts filled with dread at what they might
find in the mud.

There was a tap at the door. It couldn't be them back
yet. But the face that peeped round the crack was the
thin face of old Jacko. He was dripping wet, but walked
with confidence into the room. 'Missy Eve, I know there
is trouble at the village. I come to help.'

'Oh, Jacko.' Eve was touched by his loyalty. 'Anya,
can you find him some dry clothes? I'm sure Andrew—
Dr Craig—has some that might fit.'

'Yes, Missy. Come with me, Jacko. *Mari kita pergi*.

'And give him something to eat.'

Anya brought him back, duly dried out and dressed in
a pair of Andrew's jeans and a short-sleeved shirt. His
arms were more like sticks, but his eyes were bright, and
he was determined to help. Anya brought in a plate of
chapatis and some pieces of home-made cheese, and the
three of them sat at the table, their eyes glued on the
road through the open door as they nibbled at the food
and waited as the clock ticked away one hour, and then
two.

It was in fact Jacko who first saw the lights. He jumped
up with an exclamation and then rushed down the steps
into the rain, the women following. Andrew was leading
the way, his face and clothes smeared with mud, as he
came into the circle of light from the veranda. Behind
him strode Balik, and in his arms was a limp form,
held close against his breast. Eve mouthed the word,
'Lisa?' They came nearer, across the drain, and she
saw who it was. The words came out as a sob. 'Oh, Lisa,
Lisa!'

Andrew reached her and grasped her hands tightly.
She looked into his eyes, felt his hands tremble with the
reaction. 'She's going to be all right.'

Eve wanted to throw her arms around his neck. But

she was a nurse first, a woman second. 'What can I do?'

'Just get her into a clean dry bed and keep her warm.'

'Thank God you got there in time.' They were through in the ward now, and Eve deftly laid Lisa on an old towel, drying her as well as she could and replacing her soaked clothes with a clean cotton nightdress. Lisa moaned and stirred, but did not regain consciousness. There was an abrasion on the side of her head, which Eve was bathing with antiseptic when Andrew came back, himself clean and dry. Eve said, 'Was there no one else?'

'The driver. He was conscious and said he didn't need to go to hospital. He's staying in the village.'

'And Lisa?' Eve put a dry dressing on the wound and smoothed the damp hair on the pillow.

'Concussion, I think. She took a little water.'

Balik came in. The animosity between the two men had vanished. He looked down at the pale face and closed eyes of his precious cargo. 'Thank God. We were just in time, Eve. We almost missed the place where she was lying. She had banged her head. Andrew said she would not have survived the night.' There were tears of relief pouring down the smooth olive cheeks, and he did not try to hide them as he bent and pressed a sudden kiss on Lisa's limp hands. Eve stole a glance at Andrew. He would surely not appreciate such open affection from his rival. But the doctor appeared unconcerned, only taking Lisa's hand after Balik had finished with it, and feeling the pulse again.

'Is it normal?'

'Better. Much better.' He stretched his slim body, bending back to ease aching shoulders. 'It is only exhaustion. She will sleep it off. I checked her thoroughly before we moved her. I must say, that cab driver deserves some sort of medal. He pulled her out, when the whole thing was upside down in a drain and oozing with mud.'

'Don't.' Eve could stand most things, but her imagination had been with poor Lisa all the time, and she almost felt as though she had been through the same ordeal. She said to the men, 'I'll stay with her tonight. You two look as though you could use some rest.'

Balik spoke, his voice firm with a new authority. 'I'll stay with her, Eve. I want to.' Again, Eve turned to Andrew. For some reason, he was looking at her.

'Well, I don't mind. But you'd better get a shower and something to eat first.'

'No.' His face was strained, but the maturity in his tone was unmistakable. For a happy-go-lucky young man, Mr Balik was suddenly presenting some surprises.

'You'd frighten the life out of her if she woke and saw all that mud on your face.'

'I'll stay.' And this time there was a note of anger in his voice. Eve said no more, merely nodding and preparing to give up her seat at the bedside. Just then there was a slight moan and Lisa stirred, turning her head from side to side. Eve bent and whispered, 'You are all right, Lisa. You are home. Rest now.'

The almond eyes flickered and opened. For a moment she lay, bemused. Then she turned and recognised Eve. A slow smile lit her face to an ethereal beauty, despite the ugly bruise and the sticking-plaster. 'I made it.' Her voice was husky.

It was Balik who answered. 'You made it, Lisa, thank God.'

She looked past Eve and recognised him. 'Balik!' She reached out a hand and he clasped it tightly, tears again in his eyes. 'Balik, I—' but she forgot what she was going to say, and had slipped away into sleep before she could finish her sentence.

There was a hoarse whisper from the bed in the corner. 'She going to be all right?'

Eve stood up. 'Yes, Danny. You can all sleep well tonight.' She touched Balik's shoulder. 'Shall I bring you something to eat?'

He was still holding her hand. 'If you like. How often shall I check her pulse?'

'Hourly. But I'll be coming through to do her blood pressure.' Eve felt her own head begin to nod with weariness. She took Lisa's pulse once more and checked her temperature. Normal. There was no fever. She would soon recover from this night's ordeal. Eve went to the alcove and lay down on the spare bed where Anya often slept. She was soon asleep, leaving the two men who loved Lisa together at her bedside.

She woke periodically to check her patient. Balik did not move from his place beside her. Andrew had slept in the chair at the desk, his head on his arms. The third time Eve woke, he prevented her from getting up. 'I'll go,' he whispered. 'Get some rest now.' And she saw him pick up the sphig and gently take the slim brown arm into his capable fingers to check her blood pressure while she still slept. Neither Lisa nor Balik stirred as he did this, and Eve watched him stop at the foot of the bed and look down in an almost fatherly fashion at the two of them fast asleep, their hands clasped together. If she were looking for signs of a passionate attachment on the part of Andrew, he was certainly not showing it.

At six, Anya brought in a tray of refreshing tea for them all. And in a glorious sign that all was well, the first rays of sun thrust out from cracks in the ragged black clouds that had drifted away to the east. Balik rubbed his eyes, his face still streaked with dry mud. Eve said gently, 'Come on, Balik. Have a quick shower. You know she is all right now.'

He stretched his back and arms. 'I will go as soon as she is awake, and I know for sure she is well.'

Lisa said softly from the pillow, her eyes still closed, but her lips smiling, 'I am well. I am quite well.'

Balik's was the broadest grin Eve had ever seen him give. 'Then sit up, woman, and have some tea.'

Lisa did not open her eyes, but said, 'It is Anya's tea. My favourite. Now I know I am home.'

'Yes, your favourite. And if you are not up in two seconds, I am going to drink it. Stop teasing me and open your eyes.'

Lisa did as she was told, lifting herself on the pillows without any help. Balik held out the teacup. 'But what do I get for giving it to you?'

Lisa looked around the bed. Eve and Andrew stood at the foot. Anya was opposite Balik. And even young Danny had limped from his bed to greet the pretty invalid with a friendly handshake. She said, in her musical accent, 'I am not sure who to thank first.' She looked up at Andrew. 'I am sure you must have saved me.' She held out a hand to him. Eve watched as Andrew came to her, took the hand, and bent to kiss it.

'Welcome back,' was all he said, and stood back at once.

'I owe you my life.'

He shook his head. 'Not only me. Balik was the one who got you out, while the villagers helped me to hold up the car with ropes. And he was the one who carried you all the way back.' Andrew smiled at her. 'And he has stayed with you all night, too. Are you going to thank him?'

With a slight flush, Lisa turned to Balik and kissed him lightly on the cheek. He handed over the tea with a smile. 'Now I will go and wash off some of this mud.'

'I'll come with you, Balik. You'll need to borrow some

fresh clothes.' And the two men went off together, weary, but elated by the successful outcome of their efforts.

Eve sat and talked to Lisa while they both ate some breakfast. Then Eve made Lisa rest again, promising that she could get up in the afternoon. She looked back at the gentle soul, who was already sleep again, as her body regained its strength. It was so hard to tell—did she and Andrew have any special relationship? It had certainly not looked like it—except for that chivalrous kiss and the affectionate look that passed between them. Eve sighed, and went up to her own room to get her towel and go across the yard to the shower.

Refreshed and glowing, she returned to her room, only to find that Anya had done no washing. The sarong she had been wearing was dirty. Her uniform was crumpled at the bottom of the wardrobe. She shook her head in disbelief. Did she consider herself well-organised, when she didn't have a thing to wear? The only dress she possessed that was fit to wear was the silk sarong the Sultana had given her. She put it on, hastily gathering up the clothes that needed washing and taking them down to the kitchen. 'I do them right away,' smiled Anya. 'But Missy Eve, you look lovely today.'

'I dare say—but even *I* don't think that this is quite suitable to take a clinic. How soon will my uniform be ready?'

'I do it first,' promised Anya.

After quickly checking that all was well in the ward, and that Zaina was there, being told all that had happened by the faithful Jacko, Eve went out to the veranda. She might have known that Andrew was there, by the fragrance of coffee newly ground. 'There is a cup for you, Eve.'

She walked slowly out at his invitation, gazing as

though on a world she had never seen before, for the
welcome sun poured down on the fresh, clean trees, and
twinkled on the rippling water in the monsoon drain.

'What a jewel of a morning.'

'My words exactly.' But Andrew was looking at Eve,
not the brilliance of the sky, as the mist rose quickly from
the trees into the deep blue vastness above the fringed
palms.

She turned as he brought her a cup of coffee, and they
stood together looking out, drinking in the warm beauty
as well as their coffee. 'I suppose everyone will be out
this morning, checking the damage and repairing what
the rain washed away,' she said quietly.

He nodded, taking the empty cups to the table. 'And
I'll be taking a trip along to the highway. Every time it
rains like this, my brake discs get rusty unless I take her
out for a spin right away.' He paused. 'Will you come
along for the ride?'

'I'd like to.' Then she thought of her patients. 'We
won't be too long, will we? I must make sure Danny gets
home today. And there's Misra. You did say he ought to
go to Jahin for tests?'

'Come on, come on, Eve, relax! We'll do that when
we get back.' She detected a note of irritation. Was it
because of Lisa? Eve did not dare to ask. They walked
down towards the cars. Eve's van looked cleaner. The
Rover was next to it, and Balik's scarlet Toyota parked
crookedly at the end. As they passed the Toyota,
Andrew patted the roof. 'Quite a character, that young
man.'

'Yes.'

Andrew turned so that she had to look into his face.
'Are you very fond of him, Eve?'

They had reached the Rover, and Eve walked round
it, so that she faced him across the roof of the dark green

car. She said lightly, 'He's a nice guy, I told you before.'

'But more than that? You saw how he and Lisa—'

'Yes, I saw. And I'm delighted for them. His cheerfulness will be ideal for her shyness—and her grace will soon calm down his clowning a little.'

Andrew's tone darkened. 'You mean to say that you don't care for him—that the little act you put on was for my benefit? To keep me at arm's length?'

She wasn't sure how to answer him. 'In a way, I suppose—'

'In a way I suppose!' he imitated her angrily. 'And what does that mean? You used him as a barrier to me—just as you used Mike Grant. Just as you are using this car at this very moment. You couldn't make it any clearer, lass, if you spelled it out in words of one syllable. Keep away from me, Andrew Craig!'

Her feelings shaken, Eve answered him in a similar tone. 'And why do you think I did it, Andrew Craig? You don't think I enjoyed finding excuses not to fall in love, do you? I just didn't want to get hurt, that's all. It's a perfectly natural thing to do.'

'And why on earth would you get hurt? When I told you plainly how I felt about you, how I admired you and couldn't stop thinking of you, how I'd never met anyone like you. Why run away from that?' His voice changed then, and he spoke very softly. The birds in the jungle were chirruping their joy at the return of the sun, and the grasshoppers were chirping in the grass all around them. 'Eve, you were never out of my mind. How in heaven I stopped myself sometimes from storming into your room and forcing you to make love to me, I'll never know. I've lain awake at night, imagining you lying there, wishing with all my heart that we could be together. Is there something wrong with me, lass, that you kept on avoiding me like that, driving me insane?'

Her heart was singing crazily as she listened to his words. She edged her way round the bonnet of the Rover and went and stood close beside him, her eyes downcast. 'It sounds—illogical, I suppose. Do you really want to know?' He put his hands on her shoulders and waited until she looked up at him. Then he nodded. 'Well, Lisa was away. I thought it would be wrong. I thought that you and she—that there was some sort of understanding between you.'

His voice was very low now. 'The only reason Lisa and I like each other is because I only came here once in one or two weeks. We hardly ever exchanged any conversation apart from work.'

'I didn't get that impression.'

'And so you invented reasons to keep us apart? But you do like me a little?' His hands were still on her shoulders. She put her arms around his waist and laid her cheek against his chest by way of answer. The beating of his heart was loud in her ear. His grip tightened around her. 'Tell me, Eve.'

'You were never out of my mind. How I stopped myself from storming into your room and forcing you to make love to me, I'll never know.' She quoted his words back at him, her voice muffled because she was hiding her face in his shirt.

He tilted her face upwards then, and kissed her lips lightly, and again, forcing them apart in a kiss that almost took her breath away. He drew away only to say, 'Don't stop yourself tonight, lass, will you? I'll be waiting.'

'Doctor, Doctor!' They both turned towards the village road. A woman was trudging along, supporting a limping old man who was clutching at his stomach. 'Oh, help me, Tuan. The Bomoh, he make the spell on me,' he begged.

Andrew stepped forward. 'The Bomoh cannot make spells. I doubt if he can even make water! He's completely barmy, my man.' Eve had a smile as the man approached. Then she saw that the woman with him was old Haria. 'If there is anything wrong with you, it will be entirely medical, I assure you.'

Haria agreed vocally. 'Yes, yes, you are right, *baiklah*, Doctor, *baiklah*.' She turned towards Eve. 'Jacko, he tell us everything about the Bomoh. He tell us that you and Sister Carrol, you have the best, powerful medicine in the world. All village agree with Jacko now, Sister Carrol. They know Bomoh is the silly fellow.'

The man was more grudging. 'Yes, your medicine powerful. But the Bomoh, he make my stomach come out of the hole.' And he pulled down his sarong to reveal a very obvious inguinal hernia.

'Lie down.' The man obliged, and Andrew's capable fingers eased the hernia gently, until it slipped back inside the muscle wall. 'Wait a moment. Don't move yet. You see? Nothing to do with the Bomoh. Just a little weakness of the abdominal muscles.'

'Shall I fetch an abdominal support?'

Andrew looked up. 'Yes, please, Eve. And will you bring young Misra out? As we are going to Jahin anyway, we might as well take this patient as well and turn ourselves into an ambulance.'

Eve entered the ward in time to witness a touching embrace between Balik and Lisa. She watched them for a moment, unobserved. They had certainly complicated her life—but she knew she had done the right thing. If she had given herself to Andrew, she would never really have known how deeply he did think of Lisa. Now she had seen the evidence with her own eyes. Andrew loved her, she knew, as powerfully and as sincerely as she did him. It might be only the Indian sparrows warbling away

in the jungle out there, but to Eve, it was an angel
chorus. She felt as though she were floating, as she went
to the appliance cupboard and brought out an elastic
stomach bandage. Balik noticed her and moved frac-
tionally away from Lisa. Eve smiled. 'Don't move on my
account. I'm sure that where Lisa is concerned, no
doctor could do more good than you are doing.'

She helped Misra to his feet and told Zaina to take
Danny home. Misra had few possessions, and they were
soon collected in a small canvas bag. 'I will get well
soon?' he asked, as they walked slowly back to the car.

'I am convinced of it. You will have to take the drugs
we have given you for a long time. But they will keep you
well.'

There was a shout behind them, and Balik came
running after them. He held out his old guitar. 'Here,
Misra. You have this. My fiancée has offered to buy me a
new one.'

Misra's face glowed with delight. 'For me? *Terimasakih, encik* Balik.'

Eve reached out and shook Balik's hand. 'Congratulations. Don't get married before we get back for lunch.'

He shook his head with his famous grin. 'Can't promise.'

They reached the car. Andrew grabbed her waist.
'You were away too long,' he murmured in her ear,
before reaching out to help put Misra's bag and guitar in
the boot.

'Now, you'll want Mr Baharu to lie down in the back,
won't you?' Eve looked down at the patient who still lay
on the grass, propped against a tree trunk.

Haria looked at the Rover. 'You want that I come
with Mr Baharu?'

Andrew shook his head. 'No, Haria. Just let his family
know that I'm taking him to Jahin to see a surgeon at the

hospital. And Haria—we are very glad to hear that the people in Dantang are going to be good to Sister Carrol from now on.'

'Oh yes, Doctor. Now Jacko tell us good, we know the Bomoh will only talk rubbish to us.' And she turned and started off back to the village.

Andrew said, 'She means it, Eve. You've won the people over by your own kindness—your own good nursing, if you like. And you deserve all the praise you will be given. To them Jacko was dead. You've just done a miracle.'

She smiled into his blue eyes, feeling that she was almost drowning in her own happiness. Wherever he was, they would always look at each other now with that secret look. And there would be no need of words.

'You—take me all the way to the hospital?' Mr Baharu did not believe that he was getting such presidential treatment.

'Yes. Hold on to your stomach, and hop in the back— well, crawl in then.' Andrew's spirits sparkled like the sun on the water in the monsoon drain. 'You next, Misra.'

Eve said, 'Wouldn't it be better if Misra sat in the front, with the safety belt?

'And where would you sit, lass? You weren't thinking of staying here, were you? It is no use me going to buy a gold ring if I haven't got the finger with me to try it on.'

Mr Baharu was still puzzled why these two kind people appeared to be so extremely happy about giving him and his hernia a lift into Jahin.

Doctor Nurse Romances

Amongst the intense emotional pressures of modern medical life, doctors and nurses often find romance. Read about their lives and loves in the other three Doctor Nurse titles available this month.

SIGH FOR A SURGEON
by *Lynne Collins*

Lorimer women are not to be trusted! Betrayed by one Lorimer six year ago, surgeon Griff Rydell has neither forgotten nor forgiven his suffering. And when theatre nurse Kelly Lorimer appears at Porthbryn General, he makes it quite clear that this time he's *not* going to fall under the family spell . . .

A TIME TO HEAL
by *Sarah Franklin*

Impervious to feminine charms — that's the rumour about surgeon Stuart Lyndon. Which is fine by Lisa Dawson, his quiet and reserved scrub nurse, who steers well clear of personal relationships. So why is it that of all the willing nurses at St Jude's it's *she* who catches Mr Lyndon's eye?

NURSE IN WAITING
by *Janet Ferguson*

Forced by injury to take a break from nursing, Thea Westering counts herself lucky to land a secretarial job on St Stephen's orthopaedic ward. And even luckier to work with attractive registrar James Mayling . . .

Mills & Boon
the rose of romance

Mills & Boon

4 Doctor Nurse Romances
FREE

Coping with the daily tragedies and ordeals of a busy hospital, and sharing the satisfaction of a difficult job well done, people find themselves unexpectedly drawn together. Mills & Boon Doctor Nurse Romances capture perfectly the excitement, the intrigue and the emotions of modern medicine, that so often lead to overwhelming and blissful love. By becoming a regular reader of Mills & Boon Doctor Nurse Romances you can enjoy EIGHT superb new titles every two months plus a whole range of special benefits: your very own personal membership card, a free newsletter packed with recipes, competitions, bargain book offers, plus big cash savings.

AND an Introductory FREE GIFT for YOU.
Turn over the page for details.

Fill in and send this coupon back today and we'll send you

4 Introductory
Doctor Nurse Romances yours to keep

FREE

At the same time we will reserve a subscription to Mills & Boon Doctor Nurse Romances for you. Every two months you will receive the latest 8 new titles, delivered direct to your door. You don't pay extra for delivery. Postage and packing is always completely Free. There is no obligation or commitment — you receive books only for as long as you want to.

It's easy! Fill in the coupon below and return it to
MILLS & BOON READER SERVICE, FREEPOST, P.O. BOX 236, CROYDON, SURREY CR9 9EL.

Please note: **READERS IN SOUTH AFRICA write to Mills & Boon Ltd., Postbag X3010, Randburg 2125, S. Africa.**

- -

FREE BOOKS CERTIFICATE

To: Mills & Boon Reader Service, FREEPOST, P.O. Box 236, Croydon, Surrey CR9 9EL.

Please send me, free and without obligation, four Dr. Nurse Romances, and reserve a Reader Service Subscription for me. If I decide to subscribe I shall receive, following my free parcel of books, eight new Dr Nurse Romances every two months for £8.00, post and packing free. If I decide not to subscribe, I shall write to you within 10 days. The free books are mine to keep in any case. I understand that I may cancel my subscription at any time simply by writing to you. I am over 18 years of age.
Please write in BLOCK CAPITALS.

Name _____

Address _____

_____

_____ Postcode _____

SEND NO MONEY — TAKE NO RISKS

EP